The Dancer from the Dance

A New Sherlock Holmes Mystery

Note to Readers:

Your enjoyment of this new Sherlock Holmes mystery will be enhanced by re-reading the original story that inspired this one —

The Adventure of the Dancing Men.

It has been appended and may be found in the back portion of this book.

The Dancer from the Dance

A New Sherlock Holmes Mystery #30

Craig Stephen Copland

Published by:

Conservative Growth Inc.
3104 30th Avenue, Suite 427
Vernon, British Columbia, Canada
V1T 9M9

Cover design by Rita Toews
ISBN-10:   1721834087
ISBN-13: 978-1721834082

:

O chestnut tree, great rooted blossomer,
Are you the leaf, the blossom or the bole?
O body swayed to music, O brightening glance,
How can we know the dancer from the dance?

William Butler Yeats, from *Among School Children*

Contents

Acknowledgements

All writers of Sherlock Holmes stories owe a great debt of gratitude to Arthur Conan Doyle. The multitude of plots and characters found in the sixty stories of The Canon provide our limited imaginations with infinite sources of inspiration for the creation of new adventures for Sherlock Holmes.

The landmark annotated editions of the stories and the never-ending stream of articles—from whimsical to scholarly—about Holmes, Doyle, the canonical stories, and life in the Victorian/Edwardian era combine to make research for any new story a source of intellectual delight.

For this particular story, I am also indebted to the rich library on the history of ballet and, in particular, the many books and articles about *Les Ballets Russes* and the impact of that exceptional company on the world of dance. While admitting my failure to pay tribute to the many short articles that can be found on the Internet and the clips and full performances on YouTube, I must acknowledge my debt to *Apollo's Angels: A History of Ballet* by Jennifer Homans, and to the volume of books and articles written about *Les Ballets Russes* and Vaslav Nijinsky by Joan Acocella, the reigning doyen of American dance critics.

For over half a century, the notes giving Nijinsky's chorography instructions for *Le Sacre du Printemps* were lost.

Diligent research by Millicent Hodson led to the faithful recreation of the original performance. It was first performed by the Joffrey Ballet company and it was their rendition that I relied on for this story. I also made use of Rudolph Nureyev's version of *Après Midi d'un Faune* in describing that ballet in the story. Both of the above can be found on YouTube.

Again, I thank my two closest editors and critics, my wife, Mary Engelking and my brother, Dr. James Copland, for their long-suffering task of encouraging me in this project while at the same time ruthlessly correcting my mistakes and my tendency to run on and on. My cluster of Beta Readers are, as always, invaluable, as have been my friends and colleagues in the Buenos Aires English Writers Critique Group who meet weekly and tell me what is wrong with every chapter.

And finally, if it were not for the oddball family of us Sherlockians throughout the world who buy and enjoy yet another story about Sherlock Holmes, there would be no purpose in writing them.

CSC, Buenos Aires, June 2018

Welcome to New Sherlock Holmes
Mysteries –

"The best-selling series of new Sherlock
Holmes stories. All faithful to The Canon."

Each story is a tribute to one of the sixty
original stories about the world's most famous
detective. If you are encountering these new
stories for the first time, start with *Studying
Scarlet*, and keep going.
(https://www.amazon.com/dp/B07CW3C9YZ)

If you subscribe to Kindle Unlimited,
then you can 'borrow for free' every one of
the books.

They are all available as ebooks,
paperbacks, hardcovers, and in large print.

Check them out at
www.SherlockHolmesMysteries.com.

Welcome to New Sherlock Holmes Mysteries –

"The best-selling series of new Sherlock Holmes stories. All faithful to The Canon."

Each story is a tribute to one of the sixty original stories about the world's most famous detective. If you are encountering these new stories for the first time, start with *Studying Scarlet,* and keep going. (https://www.amazon.com/dp/B07CW3C9YZ)

If you subscribe to Kindle Unlimited, then you can 'borrow for free' every one of the books.

They are all available as ebooks, paperbacks, hardcovers, and in large print.

Check them out at www.SherlockHolmesMysteries.com.

Diligent research by Millicent Hodson led to the faithful recreation of the original performance. It was first performed by the Joffrey Ballet company and it was their rendition that I relied on for this story. I also made use of Rudolph Nureyev's version of *Après Midi d'un Faune* in describing that ballet in the story. Both of the above can be found on YouTube.

Again, I thank my two closest editors and critics, my wife, Mary Engelking and my brother, Dr. James Copland, for their long-suffering task of encouraging me in this project while at the same time ruthlessly correcting my mistakes and my tendency to run on and on. My cluster of Beta Readers are, as always, invaluable, as have been my friends and colleagues in the Buenos Aires English Writers Critique Group who meet weekly and tell me what is wrong with every chapter.

And finally, if it were not for the oddball family of us Sherlockians throughout the world who buy and enjoy yet another story about Sherlock Holmes, there would be no purpose in writing them.

CSC, Buenos Aires, June 2018

NEW SHERLOCK HOLMES MYSTERIES

Chapter One

A Murder in the West End

"Dancers," observed Sherlock Holmes one late November afternoon, "are just like all other artists. Only ... more so. Unlike the rest of us who merely strut and fret our hour upon the stage, these young men and women display spectacular beauty, form, and athleticism as they gracefully leap and pirouette across the stages of the West End. They are artists of the highest degree, utterly, intensely devoted to and passionate about their art. Their burning passion possesses them not only on the stage but also in every aspect of their bodies and souls. It can be observed in their walk, their speech, their dress, their love lives, their friendships and animosities, and their politics.

"Unfortunately," he continued after lighting his beloved pipe, "it can also be seen in the way, from time to time, they murder each other."

By the late autumn of 1913, when the strange case if *The Dancer from the Dance* took place, Sherlock Holmes and I were no longer young men. Several decades had passed since that day we met as callow young fellows with our adult lives still in front of us and agreed to share lodgings for no other reason than our parlous financial situations. Between us, we did not have two spare farthings to rub together and no means of reliable income.

Now, we are somewhat comfortably well off. Holmes has been the recipient of more awards and rewards than even his prodigious memory can keep track of. For several years now, he has been retired from his detective work and spends most of his time in Sussex, attending to his bees. However, from time to time, he is drawn out of retirement when a compelling case calls on his unique talents.

I, long ago, substantially reduced my hours at my medical practice and pursued a splendid life as a well-paid writer. We are recognized when walking the streets of London, and we play our role as sixty-year-old smiling public men, expected to deliver wise saws and modern instances.

I am often asked to reflect on the past decades of my life and declare which period of time I consider to have been "the best." The question, of course, is impossible to answer unless the asker is highly specific and phrases it as "the best for *what*?" My days in the military were definitely not the best for anything, but it was my poverty and ill health at the end of those days that led me into my friendship with Sherlock Holmes, and so, for that wonderful result, I must be grateful. My early years as Holmes's companion were intense, uncertain, dangerous, and wonderful. Those were the days when together we tracked down Jefferson Hope and Jonathan Small, when Holmes was bested by *the* woman, Irene Adler, and when he sorted out the complicated cases of Jabez Wilson, Mary Sutherland, James McCarthy and the lovely Mrs. Neville St. Clair. It was also the time when I met my first true love, Mary Morstan, and married her. For all those reasons, those early years were good, for *me*.

But what of the rest of mankind?

If I stand back and look at the past, I have to conclude that the all-too-brief years in the early part of the second decade of the twentieth century—before the world descended in the hell of war—were the best any of us can remember. Perhaps they are the best that will ever be.

A new king, George V, had ascended the throne, and the British Empire had brought peace, prosperity, the rule of law, and the faith of Christendom to over one-quarter of the earth's population. The nations of Europe were no longer in conflict with each other, and the free flow of capital, goods, and labor gave a boost to the wealth and well-being of all. The rising tide indeed lifted all boats. Science and the application of science to industry meant that experiences, travel, possessions, and health that a generation earlier had been confined to the rich were now within the grasp of a thrifty working man. It was a time of undeniable *progress*, so much so that even the dour theologians were convinced that we had entered the Millennium. These were the final golden years of the Golden Age.

It was also an era in which the arts and letters of Western Civilization exploded with a plenitude of music, painting, sculpture, architecture, research, poetry, creative writing, and, last but not least, dance.

It was this something of a late-comer to the world of the fine arts, dance, that was the focus of the highly unusual case that occupied the genius of Sherlock Holmes during the late autumn of 1913 and the details of which I am now putting to account.

As readers of my records of the cases of Sherlock Holmes will recall, he was quite an accomplished violin player and an enthusiastic musician. The poetic and contemplative part of his spirit led him to a singularly extensive knowledge of the symphony and the opera. Yet his knowledge of dance and specifically ballet remained superficial at best, as was mine. To some extent, this lack was understandable. Prior to 1910, dance was enjoyed mainly within the music halls and on a vulgar and unrefined level. That all changed when *Les Ballets Russes* came first to Paris and then to London.

The involvement of Sherlock Holmes in this rarefied world of the world's finest ballet dancers began on a morning in late November with a phone call to 221B. He had kept the rooms as his *pied-à-terre* for those occasions when he visited London and usually asked me to join him when he did so. I was in the familiar front room when the call came, and I answered it.

"Hello, Watson. Lestrade calling. Where's Holmes?"

"And good morning to you as well, Chief Inspector. He is currently here but deep into his reading the latest on apiarian science. Shall I have him ring you back later? Perhaps this afternoon?"

"No. You can tell him to get himself over to Drury Lane on the double. Corner of Martlett Court. And I mean now."

"Perhaps you would like me to interrupt him, and you can speak to him directly?"

"No, Doctor, I would not. The last thing I need this morning is to endure a round of his arrogance. That is your job. So, you tell him, and I will see him there within half an hour. You should come too."

He hung up.

I looked at Holmes, who was smiling back at me and had already turned off the gas and was placing his test tubes and instruments back in their rack.

"I could hear Lestrade across the room," he said. "This experiment was going nowhere, and we might as well go and see what the old boy is up to."

The days of the Hansom cab were long gone, and we hailed a motor car that was designated as a taxi. The traffic was light, and we made our way along Marylebone, Euston, and Gower in just over twenty minutes. Our old accomplice, now the Chief

Inspector of Scotland Yard, was standing on the corner waiting for us.

"They are back here," he said as he turned and started walking into Martlett Court.

"And who might *they* be," asked Holmes, directing his question to the back of Lestrade's head.

"Two dead people. Who do you think? I would not call you in and put up with you if I were dealing with pickpockets. But no way to identify them. Local shopkeepers do not recognize them at all. Nobody heard anything."

A cluster of police officers was standing in the middle of the lane not far in front of us. Through the forest of their legs, I could see two bodies lying prone on the pavement. By their clothing, one was a man and the other a woman.

"Has the site been disturbed?" asked Holmes.

"Good lord, Holmes," said Lestrade. "You have been asking me that question for over thirty years. Of course, it has not been disturbed. Not that it makes much difference. They were not killed here. No blood anywhere except on the backs of their heads where they were shot. Must have been robbed and killed somewhere else and dumped here."

Holmes and I knelt down and carefully examined the two victims. They were both slender and dressed in the height of fashion. The residue of gunpowder on the backs of their skulls and their collars indicated that they had been shot at close range.

We gently rolled them over so we could look at their faces. Both were young and quite attractive, with firm, tight bodies. Holmes conducted an examination of their musculature, facial features, and hands. He removed their shoes and, using his glass, observed their feet. Then he stood up.

"There is a Russian ballet troupe currently in London, is there not? They will be short two dancers for future performances."

"Holmes," said Lestrade, "would you mind terribly explaining how you know that?"

"It could not be more obvious, Inspector. Their faces announce to the world that they are Slavs. Shaped, if you can use your imagination, as if by the forceful application of heavy frying pans."

"Holmes," said Lestrade. "I am not in the mood."

"It is common knowledge, my dear inspector. Whereas the English race is characterized by singularly unattractive puffy faces, untouched by any force of nature, those from the northern part of the Continent have longer, thinner faces, as if two frying pans were firmly smacked together, one to each side of the face, like a pair of cymbals. These two faces are passably attractive but round and lean. It is as if the frying pans were applied one directly to the front, giving them the flattened features and wide-spread eyes, and the other to the top of the head, reducing the height of frontal dome to a mere two inches. Their features announce that they have come from somewhere east of Warsaw. Both the man and the woman have exceptionally hard and highly developed calves, quadriceps, hamstrings, and gluteals. The man's arms and shoulders are likewise strong and firm, but the woman's arms are willowy. Their clothes are somewhat Bohemian in style but expensive. Thus, I conclude that they are from Russian and ballet dancers."

"Good lord, Holmes," said Lestrade. "London is lousy with Russian immigrants now. Half of them ride bicycles."

"Quite so, Inspector. However, if you examine the feet of the woman, you will see that her toes are compacted and bruised. Neither bicyclists nor any other type of athlete bear these marks. On the male, there are specks of a white powder under his fingernails that has the distinct feel of resin. Male dancers apply that substance regularly so as to avoid dropping ballerinas when their hands become sweaty. Now, I have limited knowledge of the ballet, but what little I do know leads to the conclusion I have just given you. Were they carrying any travel or foreign identification documents?"

"None of that sort," said Lestrade. "The woman had nothing on her at all. The male only had some papers in the pocket of his overcoat. All their money was taken in the robbery."

Holmes sighed. "No, my dear Inspector, they were not the victims of robbery. Whoever murdered them only wanted Scotland Yard to think that."

"But their pockets were cleaned out."

"Of course, they were. But the man still has his watch and his gold cufflinks. The woman has a necklace and several expensive rings. The total value of their jewelry must be close to one hundred pounds. No thief in London today would leave those items on his victims, nor would he murder them and risk the gallows when he could easily have just taken their money and accessories and been on his way. Whatever the reason for their deaths, it was something other than the cash in their pockets."

Lestrade made a sort of grunting sound, summoned one of his police officers, and instructed him to hand over the folded set of papers he was holding.

"This is what the fellow did have in his pockets," he said.

Holmes glanced at them quickly and then gave them to me. They consisted of a single piece of paper and a booklet containing a musical score. On the front page of the score was printed the title, *Prélude à après-midi d'un faune,* underneath which was the name, *Claude Debussy.* The single page contained about twenty lines, all of which contained three numbers each. They were written in this manner:

C.G. 28 – 11 11.00

6 - 4 – x 2

7 – 13 – x 3

8 – 3 – x 9

10 – 19 – x14

"May I suggest," said Holmes, "that you take these bodies to the police morgue and that we arrange a visit immediately to whoever is in charge of the Russian dancers. If you have no objection, Inspector, I shall keep these papers for the present time."

"Fine by me," said Lestrade. "I cannot make any sense of them at all. I will have my office track down the Russians straight away and set up a meeting. You will get a call to let you know when and where. I will see you there."

Having said that, he abruptly departed and walked back out to Drury Lane, where his car and driver were waiting for him

Chapter Two

The Fabulous Impresario

Scotland Yard called in the early afternoon. A woman from Lestrade's office spoke to me in a gracious and respectful manner but stated in no uncertain terms that Holmes and I were required immediately in the lobby of the Savoy Hotel. The Chief Inspector would meet us there in half an hour.

The Savoy, in the Strand, had opened over a decade ago and was the most luxurious hotel in London. It had been the first hotel in Europe to provide every guest with his or her own lavatory, complete with a constant supply of hot and cold running water. The restaurant had become the preferred dining establishment of London's *hoi poloi,* and the rich and shameless could be seen there every evening. Lestrade was waiting for us by the front desk, accompanied by two police officers in uniform and a gentleman whom I recognized from the society pages of the press as Mr. Charles Ritz, the hotel manager. Lestrade introduced us to him.

"We value the patronage of all of our guests," said the manager. "However, the Russian dancers do have a bit of a tendency to exhibit their emotions perhaps somewhat more than an English gentleman or lady is prepared for. Hence, I thought it best that I accompany you just in case you elicit an untoward reaction from them. Their suite is on the south side of the top floor."

The electric lift—the first to be installed in London—took us to the eighth floor of the hotel. Whilst I was enjoying the ride, Holmes turned to Lestrade and queried him concerning the party we were about to meet.

"His name is *Die – og – hi – lev,*" said Lestrade, sounding out each syllable. "He's a Russian but lives now in Paris. Brought a company of Russian dancers with him a couple of years back. Said to be very risqué. The French love them, as might be expected. He comes to London each year now and puts on a few shows at the Royal Opera House or the Drury Lane. The critics here are mixed. The aesthetes adore him; the sensible ones say he and his bunch of degenerates are beyond the pale. I have never seen them perform, so I have no idea. I think he speaks a bit of English. I had one of our artists at the

Yard sketch the faces of the victims. There are rather good likenesses. No mistaking them for anyone else."

From the lift, we walked along the beautifully appointed hallway to the door of a corner suite. Lestrade gave several firm knocks on the door.

"Beat it!" came a shout from the other side. "We're busy. Go away and come back in an hour."

The voice was distinctly American. Lestrade nodded to the hotel manager, who produced his master key and opened the door. He did not follow us into the suite.

"Hey. You guys deaf or something? Out of here before you get batty-fanged. You want me to call the police?" said a fellow who was standing in the middle of the posh suite. The room was splendidly decorated with fine paintings and furniture and must have had over a dozen large vases of fresh flowers—one on every available surface. The assertive American chap was dressed in a dark double-breasted suit, with a suit jacket cut short as is the style across the Atlantic. Unlike a cultured Englishman, he did not sport a decent set of boots covered with tan spats but instead a finely tooled pair of wing-tipped brogues. His necktie was wide and appeared to have a picture of Niagara Falls embroidered on it. He looked as if he were about to continue his diatribe when he observed the two uniformed police officers enter behind us.

"Jeepers, it's the mutton-shunkers," he exclaimed. Then turning to the other man in the room, he said, "Sergy. What have you done this time? Are your kids stealing the hotel's towels again? You gotta stop lettin' them do that, Sergy. Or we're all gonna end up in the hoosgow."

He then turned to us and spoke to Lestrade. "Whatever it is, gentlemen, I am sure it will be looked after. Allow me to introduce myself. Gerry M. Coghlan is the name, and the Great White Way is the game. And who might I have the honor of addressing, my good man?"

The American fellow was apparently used to taking command of any situation in which he found himself and directing all attention to his presence. Whilst Lestrade was staring at him, still somewhat speechless, I looked at the other people in the lavish suite. I could see that Holmes was doing the same. Sitting in a large wingback chair was a handsome, mustached gentleman clad in a silk dressing gown that covered a fine cotton shirt and colorful cravat. His short boots were stylish and gleaming. In his right hand was a cigarette holder, in which the stub of a cigarette was smoldering. His smile suggested that he found the antics of the New Yorker mildly amusing.

On either end of the sofa were two boys whose age I would have put at around fifteen. The clothes they were wearing would have been appropriate on the ballet stage but hardly what was expected in a London hotel suite in the early afternoon. From the waist down, they wore only dancer's tights that outlined every muscle and bulge in their anatomy. Above the waist, they both wore a short velvet jacket that was flared out about their hips. The front of the jacket was open, exposing their lily-white chests and abdomens. They were both exceedingly attractive, although not in a way that I would call masculine and handsome. They were not saying anything but were obviously smirking, smiling at the American, and trying to suppress their giggles.

Lestrade had recovered from his bewilderment and replied to the American.

"Chief Inspector Lestrade, Scotland Yard. With me are Mr. Sherlock Holmes and Dr. Watson."

"*Bozhe moy,*" muttered the fellow in the dressing gown. The American was more loquacious.

"Sherlock Holmes? You don't mean *the* Sherlock Holmes? Boy oh boy, this is my lucky day. I hit the jackpot. First, I get a deal to bring Sergy and his company to New York, and now I meet the world's most famous detective. In person. I could not have written a better script if I tried. Wait'll they hear about this in Peoria. Did you know, Mr. Holmes, that some guy is running all over the United States of America pretending to be you onstage? Tell ya what. Why don't you come yourself and I'll get you onstage on Broadway? The crowds will go wild. Can you see it, Mr. Holmes? *The real Sherlock Holmes. Come and see the world's greatest detective combat the forces of evil.*"

As he was speaking, he slowly waved his open hand in a long sweep from left to right. I assumed that we were supposed to be imagining the lights of a marquee. He extracted a business card from his pocket and walked directly toward Holmes, extending the card.

"No," said Holmes, "I cannot see that. And if you, sir, would kindly step aside, we have business to conduct with Mr. Diaghilev." He walked past Mr. Coghlan and over toward the man sitting in the wing chair. Diaghilev rose to his feet and smiled warmly at him.

"*Godpodin* Sherlock Holmes," he said. "It is great honor to meet so much famous person. *Rad vstreche s vami.* So happy I am to have opportunity to talk with you. But please, sir. In Russia, we never have meeting on empty stomach or without exchanging toast. *Da?*"

He nodded to the boys on the sofa, who instantly sprang to their feet and grabbed two trays off of the side console, and came over to us. One tray bore small shot glasses, all filled to the brim with a clear liquid that most certainly was a select vodka. The other had a large plate of small pieces of toasted bread, slathered in caviar. Lestrade, the police officers, and I all partook eagerly. Holmes did not.

"We are not in Russia, Mr. Diaghilev," he said. "We are in London, and I prefer to conduct meetings on an empty stomach and without the interference of alcohol."

"*Bozhe moy*, how you are missing enjoyments of life. *Khorosho*, Mr. Holmes. You are free to deprive yourself, and I shall be free not to." He downed his vodka in one gulp and then consumed one of the caviar morsels. Having done so, he sat back down on his chair and gestured with his cigarette holder for us to take a seat in one of the numerous sofas and chairs that were scatted around the suite.

"It is also custom in Russia, to give small gift before engaging in business. Had I known about your visit, I should have had excellent gift to give to famous Mr. Sherlock Holmes. But I cannot give you nothing. I give all of you tickets to ballet.

Today is Sunday, so as good Christians we do not perform but we still have good time. *Poetomu*, how you say, *therefore*, we have reception this evening at Savoy. You must come. Tomorrow is *ponedel'nik*, and is dark night in West End. Next nights we do Tchaikovsky ballet, different each night, after we do *Après-midi d'un faune.* Is short piece. Friday, we do *Le Sacre du Printemps.* First time in London. Will be big event. You will like. You must accept my gift, Mr. Holmes. I am incapable to do business any other way."

I half expected Holmes to tell the impresario that he was not interested but he surprised me and graciously accepted, promising to attend the reception and the performances. He smiled at Diaghilev and thanked him. Diaghilev grinned in return.

"Is not just good for you, sir. Looks good for me to have world's great detective, famous writer, and Inspector Chief at my party. *Da?*" He laughed and downed another shot glass of vodka.

Holmes was not smiling. He gestured to the police officer who was holding the artist's sketch pad. The fellow brought it over and handed it to Holmes, who opened it and placed it in front of Mr. Serge Diaghilev.

"Can you identify this man and woman?" Holmes asked.

The Russian fellow was suave and charming, but he could not hide the flash of recognition that flickered across his face. And it was more than mere recognition. It was fear. If his face could have spoken, it would have said, "Oh, dear God, no."

He recovered his composure immediately and looked over at the American.

"Mr. Coghlan, this does not you concern. Please wait for me in hotel bar. Shall not be long."

"It's okay, Sergy. I don't mind waiting here." He was well into his third piece of caviar-laden toast. Diaghilev's response was more forceful.

"Gerry, you wait in bar. Go now."

"Okay. Whatever you say, Sergy. I will just twenty-three skidoo out of here."

The Russian then turned to the two boys on the sofa.

"*Ubiraysya otsyuda.*"

They jumped to their feet and departed into one of the adjoining bedrooms. He then looked up at Holmes with a forced smile.

"*Da konechno,* of course, I know them. These are two of my beautiful children. Tatiana and Luka. They are members of my *Ballets Russes.* They have been arrested by Scotland Yard, *da?* What wrong were they doing? *Seksom* in Poets' Corner, perhaps? They are dancers. They do these things. I will come to police station and pay fine."

"I regret to inform you, sir," said Holmes, "that if you go to the station, it will not be to pay a fine. It will be to identify the bodies of these two young people. They have been murdered."

For a moment, Diaghilev's face was blank. Then it slowly became contorted with anguish. He gave a desperate glance to

Lestrade, who nodded in confirmation. His eyes closed, and he brought his clenched fists to his face. His body slumped in his chair and began to sob uncontrollably. Over the next several minutes, first Holmes and then Lestrade attempted to have him talk to them, but it was to no avail. The man was lost in a sea of pain.

A full five minutes passed before he raised his head and spoke to us in a whisper.

"*Da*, I come to station to identify. Is possible not to tell Press? I must contact families in Russia. Both families wonderful. Trusted me to take care of children. Is possible not to tell Press until I inform families?"

"Yes," said Lestrade. "That can be arranged. But we need your help if we are to find who did this."

He looked at Lestrade and then Holmes.

"*Da*. What to know do you want? Doctor, bring vodka, *pozhaluysta*."

I took a full shot glass from the sideboard and brought it to him. He tossed it back in one gulp.

"Tell us," said Holmes, "about these two young people. Where do they come from? Did they have enemies? Were they doing anything illegal? You have over seventy people in your company. Is there anything peculiar about these two?"

"*Nyet*. They are beautiful children. Good dancers. Work hard. Not in front line but soon to be. They are friends, lovers. Maybe other dancer is jealous. All dancers are artists. They do crazy things. Tatiana come from Novgorod. My city. Good family. Father is professor. Luka from Perm. Father is mayor. Both families send them as children to St. Petersburg to Imperial Ballet. I ask them to join my *Ballets Russes*. Do anything against law in London? Maybe steal sweets or fruit. Maybe steal shoes. Dancers love new shoes."

He dropped his head back into his hands and began again to sob. A further several minutes passed before he lifted his head again.

"Please. Another favor, I must ask. Is possible not to tell other dancers in company? Not yet. They could not dance if they know this terrible thing. Only four nights left in London. This is end of season for London. Now say them Lukasha and Tanya run off on lovers' holiday. Later, we tell them bad news. Is possible?"

"We cannot promise," said Holmes, "but we will not disclose full information until after your performance on Friday. Now then, sir, pray look at these."

He removed from his suit pocket the papers that the police officer had given him earlier in the day.

"Luka had these in his pocket," said Holmes. "What can you tell me about them?"

Diaghilev looked over the documents and shrugged.

"This is score of *Le Faune* to be played by orchestra this week. Every dancer has copy. These numbers, they make no sense. Maybe leave with me and I try. *Da?*"

"*Nyet*," replied Holmes and held out his hand for the return of the papers.

"I do what you want. We go now to station. I do what I have to do. Do not forget, you are come to reception. We all try not to look sad, *da*? Like you say, show must go on."

The group of us departed the suite and returned to the hotel lobby. The two police officers discreetly led the impresario through a back door to a waiting police car. Holmes, Lestrade and I found a table in the Savoy Grill.

"He knows more," said Lestrade, "than he's letting on."

Chapter Three

A Wisconsin Countess
at the Savoy

olmes and I met again at the end of the afternoon in 221B and relaxed in front of the hearth with a round of sherry whilst waiting for the ever-faithful Mrs. Hudson to prepare our supper. Holmes's dear landlady was now elderly but still spry and devoted to looking after her famous boarder.

"You are planning," I asked, "to speak to the other members of the company?"

He nodded.

"But you do not speak Russian," I said.

"I have called in reinforcements."

"Indeed? Who, may I ask?"

"Countess Elizaveta d'Eau Claire," he said.

"You mean Big Betsy from Wisconsin?"

"The one and only. Regardless of her eccentricities, she is a fluent native Russian speaker and always eager to assist me."

"Which I translate to mean, eager to help as long as you pay her well."

"Which I am more than happy to do. She will conduct interviews and provide translation for me as required and will accompany us to the theater. We will be attending from Tuesday through Friday. I trust you will enjoy it."

"It will be a most interesting experience," I said. "Cannot go wrong listening to Beecham conduct Tchaikovsky. He's doing *The 1812* as well, isn't he? And the Russians are performing both *Swan Lake* and *The Nutcracker*, right? Yes, that should be quite enjoyable, even if the new ballet is a bit of a way down queer street."

"More than a bit," said Holmes, "Friday may be a somewhat novel experience."

"Oh, yes, indeed. Then we shall have to sit through *The Rite of Spring.* Is not that the one that drove the French to riot when it was first performed a few months back in Paris?"

"Of course the French staged a riot. What would anyone have expected? They are French and are always either on strike or staging a riot."

"How do you think it will be received by Londoners?" I asked.

"We will listen in silence, give polite applause, and complain about it for years afterward. We are English. That is what we do."

I might have challenged his ethnographic generalizations but was interrupted by the bell at the door on Baker Street.

Mrs. Hudson appeared a moment later and handed Holmes a gilt-edged card.

"The Countess has come for a visit," she said. "You are welcome to ask her to stay for supper, but there might not be enough food for you and the doctor if she fills her plate first."

She gave me a wink and departed to fetch one of Holmes's favorite informants.

"Sheeerlock ... daaaahlink!" said the woman who appeared in our doorway. "*Bozhe moy,* and Doctor Watson. Two of my favorite men in all the world. How lovely of you, my dear, to ask me to call on you. Are we going to Simpson's for dinner, darlink? Or shall we be dining here in elegant privacy? Your dear Mrs. Hudson is such a divine chef. Not quite up to my lovely Pierre at the Savoy but makes up for it in her devotion to you. How are you anyway, dahlink?"

The woman who had entered the room and who bore the legal name of Betsy Burkovsky was of the same vintage as Holmes and me and, like a fine wine, had become more fabulous with each passing year. She was wearing an ermine stole, a gigantic hat, and a gown that provided enough yards of fine cloth to flatter her ample endowments. Under her arm, she swaddled a dog that was about the size of a well-fed rat. Upon entering the room, she immediately put the tiny beast down on the floor.

"There you go, Pépé," she said as the pathetic excuse for a canine scampered away. "Go and explore, but try not to leave an indiscretion on the carpet. Ah, Sherlock, my dearest. How sweet of you to ask for my help. I do so love rescuing you one more time. Well, frankly, I love the way I live for two weeks after you pay me for rescuing you. What is it you need this time, dahlink? An introduction to a member of the Czar's household? London is utterly crawling with the excrescence of St. Petersburg. You would think they were fleeing Russia for their lives. Or do you need to know who has been smuggling sable stoles into London? Do tell me, dahlink?"

"Translation services."

"Translation? That is all? Sherlock, my sweet man, any one of a thousand poor Russian students can translate for you. Who is it you have to speak to? The third mate from a Russian fishing trawler?"

"The members of *Les Ballets Russes*."

"Oooh, why didn't you say so!" She clapped her hands together in front of her massive bosom. "Well then, I must tell you the secret for interviewing any cultured Russian. You can learn *everything* you need to know by asking him ... or maybe her ... only *one* question."

She stopped, obviously expecting that we would demand to know what that question was. I did not want to disappoint her and demanded with feigned eagerness that she tell us.

"My dears, you merely look them in the eye and ask them, 'Do you prefer Tolstoy or Dostoevsky?' If they give a truthful answer, that is all you need to know. Everything else follows from that."

I complimented the Countess on her profound knowledge of Russian literature.

"*Bozhe moy,* Doctor. There is nothing at all to understanding the great literature of Mother Russia. The plots of every one of our stories can be summarized in only five words."

Again, she expected us to plead for such a revelation, and again I did not disappoint. I took out my pencil and notebook and posed myself as if ready to write down the answer.

"And what," I asked, "my dear Countess, might those five words be?"

She lifted her head and spoke to the light coming in the bay window. "They are 'And then ... it got worse.'"

Both Holmes and I laughed, and I thanked her again for such insight and wisdom. Holmes assured her that he would remember her counsel when speaking to the dancers.

"And, of course," she said, "we shall be attending the performances at the Royal Opera House?"

"For four nights running this week," said Holmes.

"*Zamechatel'no*! Preceded by dinner at Simpson's, of course. And followed by drinks and desserts at the Savoy. How lovely."

"Except for tonight," said Holmes. "We have to attend the reception for the company where we shall join with the excrescence of London."

"Brilliant! If I were only forty years younger, I would have that Serge Diaghilev on his knees, proposing marriage to me before the night is over. I am quite sure—as we used to say in Wisconsin—I could straighten the boy out. Now then, what is your dear Mrs. Hudson serving for dinner?"

    * * *

At eight o'clock that evening, Holmes, the Countess, and I met on the pavement in front of the Savoy Hotel. Lestrade had refused the invitation noting, wisely, that Chief Inspectors of Scotland Yard should not be seen in public enjoying the crumbs that fell from the tables of the principals in a case he was investigating.

A string of large, luxurious motor cars was puttering up, discharging cargoes of shirt-fronted men and beshaled and bediamonded women. In our early years together, I had to admonish Holmes on numerous occasions when he failed to conceal his contempt for, as he called them, the *crud de la crud*, who lived idly but well off the rents of their inherited lands and firms. Now, he was so famous that receiving an insult from Sherlock Holmes was worn as a badge of honor amongst this ostentatious crowd and was bragged about in the clubs of Pall Mall or the high teas of Mayfair.

We entered the hotel and were directed to the Lancaster Ballroom, where a small throng had already gathered beneath the glittering crystal chandeliers and were, as duty required, engaging in bantering inconsequence and forced laughter. Holmes moved directly to the far corner of the room, where his tall stature permitted him to survey the crowd.

"Kindly make a note," he said to the Countess and me, "of any of these pompous people who have a finger in the theater."

"Sherlock, my dearest," said the Countess, *sotto voce*, "do you think any of these lovely people could be involved in something criminal?"

"If you are asking me if one of them might have committed or commissioned murder, then *yes*. We have to start our investigation somewhere, and those connected to the victims are the logical place to begin."

"Shall we engage some of the dancers in conversation?" I asked.

"What dancers?" replied Holmes.

"Those who have been pressed into service to distribute the champagne and *hors-d'oeuvres.*"

Some twenty young men and women were attending to the refreshments of the guests. They were all clad in their ballet costumes. The lads were dressed in a similar manner to the boys we had seen earlier in Diaghilev's suite. They were wearing nothing but tights below their waists, and short, black velvet jackets, buttoned in the vicinity of their navels. The young women all bore the famous costumes of the *petits cygnes* of *Swan Lake*. Instead of skirts, they wore *tutus* that hung just shy of horizontal, exposing their legs. On their torsos, they were covered in form-fitting corsets made of thin material that hugged every mound and bulge in their young bodies. I assumed that they were all members of *Les Ballets Russes*.

"They are not dancers," said Holmes. "They are employees of the hotel who have been costumed for the occasion. That is obvious and quite unfortunate as I had been hoping to observe any signs of passionate feelings amongst them that might be strong enough to lead to murder."

"They look like dancers to me," I said in rejoinder.

"Watson. Please. Observe. Whilst they may have been selected because of their attractive faces and bodies, most of the males have legs that are positively spindly compared to a dancer's. The same is true of the females, in addition to which several of the girls are blessed with ample breasts that would topple them off balance should they attempt to stand *en point*. They are all balancing large trays on their spread palms and by experience remove champagne glasses first from one side and then the other so as not to render the tray unbalanced and crashing to the ground. Add to that the obvious observation that all of them are quite self-conscious of their grossly immodest costumes and do not appreciate being leered at by the aging Lotharios who surround them. The only reason I would have to speak to them is to advise that they meet together tomorrow morning and form a union so that they may never again be treated in such a degrading manner."

"Oh, Sherlock dahlink," said the Countess. "There is a reason you are still a bachelor. Why do you think all those noble ladies rave about attending the ballet if it is not because they are entranced by the parade of gorgeous *gluteus maximus* that prance across the stage? You are a lost cause, my dahlink. But come now, I shall introduce you to someone I see and whom I consider a dear and intimate friend. She is my fellow American."

"What," I asked her, "does she have to do with the theater?"

"She owns several of them. Her husband, may he rest in peace, had more money than God, and theaters were his playthings. She has turned them into machines for making money."

"Ah, then she must be quite popular amongst the dramatic crowd."

"*Au contraire,* my dear Doctor. She has banished the serious playwrights and actors from half of her real estate and turned the theaters into splendid music halls filled with vulgar vaudevillians. That, I fear, is where the money is to be found today. Come, we shall engage her. Do not be put off by her accent. She is American, and we cannot help what we do to your precious English language."

Chapter Four

We Meet Nijinsky

The Countess sailed across the portion of the ballroom between where we were standing and where a blonde woman of a certain age was momentarily alone, having recently disentangled herself from a cluster of similarly gowned and bejeweled dowagers.

"*Ellssieee*," cooed the Countess, and we approached the lady. "How lovely to see you again. Why, I have not seen you since Epsom, or was it the party for Henry Ford at the

American ambassador's? And ... oh my ... your gown is stunning. From the House of Worth? Did Jean-Phillipe design it for you? It is so much his style. His signature is all over it. Utterly maaavellous, my dear."

The lady was looking at the Countess in a manner that had words been attached to it might have said, "*Who is this?*" She obviously did not know who had accosted and was now gushing all over her. Our Countess carried on undaunted.

"Oh, my dear, Elsie, you must forgive me. Allow me to introduce you to my two gentlemen escorts for the evening. Really, my dear, how lucky can a lady be to have not only one but two famous gentlemen by her side for such a fabulous occasion. This is the famous writer, Dr. John Watson, the best-selling author now in the entire Empire, and this, if you can believe it, is Mr. Sherlock Holmes, and I am sure you know who he is. Gentleman, please meet my compatriot, Mrs. Elsie Cubitt of North Walsham."

Holmes, the woman, and I all said nothing, frozen momentarily on the sport. The elegant woman recovered first.

"Well, we meet again, Mr. Holmes. How nice to see you."

"Goodness, gracious," exclaimed the Countess. "You two know each other?"

"We have," said Mrs. Cubitt, "met before. Unfortunately, I was unconscious at the time, a bit of a bloody mess, and had a splitting headache. I have been told that it was thanks to you, Mr. Holmes, that I was not sent to the gallows."

"Good heavens!" said the Countess. "What did you do?"

"Murdered my husband; at least that is what the police first assumed. And then I tried, rather unsuccessfully, to murder myself. But thanks to Mr. Holmes, no charges were ever laid. A pleasure, sir, to renew your acquaintance under much more favorable circumstances than the previous occasion." The lady's facial expression changed to a smile, and she extended her hand. Holmes, remembering his manners for once, graciously accepted with a gallant bow.

"Your recovery," he said, "and your many accomplishments since that dreadful day are greatly admired."

"Yours as well, Mr. Holmes. I and every one of my friends wept when we read of your demise at the waterfall and were in ecstasy when you returned from the dead. But I had the impression that you rather disdained effete affairs like this."

"It seems, madam," said Holmes, "that I have reached the time of life where a man is required to participate in the events of the social stratum which I appear to have, in spite of my diligent efforts, attained. Thus, I find myself at this elegant event and with the pleasure of meeting you once again."

Mrs. Elsie Cubitt laughed pleasantly. "Oh my, Mr. Holmes. Who would have guessed that you had such refined and gracious manners?"

"Ah, but what can I say, my lady? There are occasions, such as when standing in front of a respected and elegant woman, that such behavior comes naturally."

She laughed merrily again. "And who would have guessed that Sherlock Holmes is such an accomplished liar." Now she laughed heartily. Holmes looked quite taken aback.

"I beg your pardon, madam!"

"Oh, my dear Mr. Holmes. I spend every working day administering funds for charities and the arts. I meet with countless do-gooders, theater impresarios, and lawyers. They smile graciously and flatter me, and then proceed to tell me all manner of lies. Surely you do not expect me to believe for a minute that Sherlock Holmes has come to a gala event at the Savoy because he enjoys doing so? I noticed you several minutes ago, standing at the edge of this room, peering over it like an eagle looking for his lunch. You are here because, as your friend, Dr, Watson, might write, *the game is afoot*. Would you deny what I am saying is true, Mr. Holmes?"

She did not give Holmes time to respond before continuing.

"However, my dear sir, your presence has just made this event so much more interesting. Now we are no longer at yet another pompous evening attended by England's parasitical nobility and those who wish they were. We are present at a party in which there is some sort of criminal activity taking place. That is so much more interesting. Positively intriguing. Now then, what could it possibly be? You cannot be here on behalf of the creditors of Mr. Diaghilev, that much I know for sure."

"Do you, madam?" asked Holmes. "May I ask you how you know that?"

"How? Because I am one of them and nobody told *me*. Serge owes me a fortune as he does several others here this evening, and *we* certainly did not hire Sherlock Holmes to

investigate where all of the money has gone. So, pray tell, Mr. Holmes, why are you here?"

Holmes did not answer her question but responded with one of his own.

"Pray tell yourself, my lady. Why, if he does not pay his bills, do you continue to allow him to use your theaters?"

That brought a hearty laugh from the woman. "Oh, my dear, dear Mr. Sherlock Holmes. You may possess the finest mind in the Empire when it comes to bringing criminals to justice, but it is apparent that you know nothing about the business of running a theater. Let me give you your first lesson. Anyone who can fill the house with rich people is welcome to put on his production. As long as we come within thirty percent of covering our costs from the ticket sales, we are satisfied. The profit is made on the truly criminal amounts we charge for champagne at the intermission, for souvenir magazines, for copies of the musical score, for anything that people who have more money than sense will buy. The profit on our concession sales allows us to live quite well, thank you very much. And Serge Diaghilev fills our houses night after night. The last thing we want is to put him in prison for non-payment of his debts."

Holmes nodded slowly. "I see. Very well, I assure you that I am not present this evening on behalf of his creditors. The truth is, madam, we are guests of Mr. Diaghilev."

"Oh! Well now, that does make it more interesting. Why would *he* want to hire a detective? Is somebody blackmailing the man? Has someone threatened to expose his utterly degenerate private life? I cannot imagine what purpose there would be in that. Perhaps if he were the Archbishop, there would be profit in blackmailing, but Serge's private life is public knowledge. He positively flaunts his young playthings in front of us. The word on the street is that any young man with a slender body is advised not to turn his back on him, for if he does, then Serge the Impresario may become Vlad the Impaler. We all know the man is depraved, and his ballets are likewise. Why do you think the English are flocking to see them? If you come to see his *Après-midi*, you will see what I mean. Are you planning to attend, Mr. Holmes?"

"I am," said Holmes, "and I look forward to seeing you there. It has been a pleasure."

He offered a shallow bow and retreated from Mrs. Cubitt. She was grinning at him as he did so.

"The lady," I said, "makes a good case for not equating the creditors of Mr. Diaghilev with his enemies."

Holmes tilted his head a bit to the side and raised an eyebrow. "Do you truly think so?" he said.

"It makes sense," I said.

"I claim," said Holmes, "neither expertise nor sufficient data concerning the business of the theater. Such instincts as I have, however, lead me to doubt what I have just been told."

"Well, my dahlink," replied the Countess, "I have no doubt that it is certainly *not* true with those creditors whose sole business is loaning Diaghilev money."

"He has been borrowing money?" asked Holmes.

"Well, dahlink, I cannot say for certain," said the Countess, "but I know of no other reason for Mr. Abraham Slainstein to be here."

She was discreetly nodding in the direction of a smallish, well-dressed man who was loading up his plate at the food table. Without further comment, she walked over to him. Holmes and I obediently followed.

"Abe, my dahlink," she said as she sidled up to the fellow. "How lovely to see you here. Have you suddenly developed a cultivated interest in the arts, dahlink? Wonders never cease."

The man did not look up from his plate of food. His answer seemed as sour as the cabbage roll on which he was gnawing.

"Hello, Betsy. You know I have no more interest in the arts than you do. I am here for the same reason you are. The food and wine are free, and the prospects for new clients are promising."

"Oh, Abe, you are always working, working, working. The day is over. Time to relax and enjoy yourself. Let me introduce you to the two gentlemen who are escorting me this evening."

He briefly looked up from his plate before returning his gaze to his free supper.

"Don't bother, Betsy. I know who they are. Just tell me why you are bringing Sherlock Holmes and Dr. Watson to a reception put on by pompous poseurs for the benefit of a bunch of Bohemian degenerates. And do not try to tell me that England's most famous detective and highest-paid writer have suddenly developed an interest in watching young men in stockings prance across the stage."

"I assure you, sir," said Holmes even though the request had been made to the Countess, "that I have no interest in either the artistic merit or the moral depravity of a ballet company. My interest has arisen only because of rumors that a criminal element that may have become attached to them."

That got the fellow's attention. He put down his full plate of delectable food and looked directly at Holmes.

"Well, now, this boring evening has suddenly become interesting. A pleasure to meet you, Mr. Holmes. I am Abraham Slainstein, and as I have some pecuniary interest in these dancers, your comment demands my attention as I would not want my investment in them to go down the drain even more than it already has."

"A pleasure to meet you, sir," said Holmes. "Am I correct in understanding that you are one of the financial backers of this artistic enterprise?"

"If by that you mean am I one of the fools that was sweet-talked by Serge Diaghilev into loaning money for his extravaganzas, you are correct. I thought he was bringing *Swan Lake* to the West End, which he does. But he also brings his afternoon of a salacious faun along with his bizarre *Rite of Spring*. And yesterday I am hearing that Nijinsky, the flying fairy, is about to cut and run. What should be a gold mine of profit appears to be a bottomless pit for expenses as long as Diaghilev is in charge. And now Mr. Sherlock Holmes is telling me that there are criminals connected somehow to my investment. Is there any more bad news you wish to tell me, Mr. Holmes, before I slit my wrists?"

"Your comment about Mr. Nijinsky is very interesting, sir," said Holmes. "Would you mind awfully explaining it to me?"

"An explanation? You need an explanation? Why do you not just ask him yourself? Here he comes now."

He nodded toward the doors of the reception room, where it was evident that someone significant had just entered. Swirling around me, I could hear the whispered name "Nijinsky" being passed from one patron to the other. As crowds do on such occasions, the inchoate mass of people began creeping and politely elbowing in the direction of the doorway. Countess Betsy turned and pushed her way through the crowd like a powerful ice-breaker. We followed in her wake.

Several indignant comments and glaring rebukes later, we found ourselves in the front line of a small circle that had surrounded a young man and an attractive woman who was firmly attached to his arm. He was surprisingly short, although strikingly handsome, with soft, refined features. He was elegantly dressed in a fine suit that I thought had been somewhat padded in the shoulders so as not to let them appear so narrow. The cut of the trousers, however, was disproportionately large and loose, indicating powerful pairs of thighs and calves.

The young man, who I concluded could be none other than Vaslav Nijinsky, the most famous male ballet dancer in the world, was not looking at all comfortable in the situation. A string of elegantly dressed women of all ages and sizes were bumping and shouldering each other to put their bodies in front of him. Once they achieved that strategic position, they were offering the poor fellow their gloved hands and speaking to him loudly, with elongated vowels, about how much they simply *adoored* his *daancing*. It was obvious that he did not understand what they were saying, and the woman, who was clinging to him like ivy to a lamppost, had her mouth a few inches from his left ear and appeared to be translating.

While she smiled graciously back at the well-wishers, he was oblivious to them. He took a few of the hands extended to him and gave the fingertips and very short shake. The rest he ignored. His eyes were wide and were darting about the room as if he were a cornered animal looking for a rapid means of escaping a predator. This odd spectacle went on for several minutes, during which the woman who was affixed to his arm steered him in a brief circle around the room. We shuffled and elbowed our way close behind. At one point, I observed that his gaze suddenly stopped flashing back and forth and had become fixed. My own glance in the direction in which he was looking revealed that Serge Diaghilev was standing in the line of sight and was looking directly back at Nijinsky. It was hard to describe what I read in the look they were giving to each other. Diaghilev was angry, but the anger seemed tinged with condescension and sadness. In Nijinsky, I read defiance but also fear. Something had transpired between the two of them, and it was far from resolved.

Holmes grabbed my elbow and, with his other hand on Betsy's arm, led us away from the madding crowd and over to the bar where we could refresh our glasses of Champagne.

"Countess," said Holmes. "Doctor Watson and I shall remain here. It is not advisable for me to encourage even more speculation regarding my presence. Would you be so kind as to mingle amongst the guests and find out, whether it is in English, Russian or Polish, just what is going on here? And then come and report back to us. I shall look after your food plate whilst you do so."

Countess Betsy smiled warmly at Holmes and plowed her way back into the crowd. Holmes discreetly worked his way to the back of the bar until he was standing beside the well-starched waiter who was tending to the libations of the gentry. He removed his wallet from his suitcoat pocket and extracted a five-pound note and slipped it into the hand of the barkeep. Without looking at each other, Holmes quietly asked questions about certain of the guests who had caught his attention. The barkeep whispered back, displaying a rather impressive knowledge of the upper crust of London. I stood behind the two of them, within earshot, and scribbled notes.

We kept up this exercise for over a half-hour. The barkeep provided extensive data, some factual and some mere gossip, concerning the various personages and pretenders on the floor.

"You see those two chaps by the wall on the left," he said. "The ones in the suits that do not fit properly?"

Our gaze was directed to two tall Slavic looking fellows standing apart from the crowd.

"I do," said Holmes. "And who, pray tell, might they be?"

"The Ambassador of Russia and his deputy, who is also the head of the Okhrana for all of Britain. They like to keep an eye on their citizens to make sure they behave themselves. And do you see the three young chaps by the food tables who are trying to fill their pockets with pieces of meat and cheese without being noticed?"

I now looked in that direction and, sure enough, noticed three young men standing with their backs to the food table. Several times as I was watching them, one of them slipped his hand behind his back, grabbed as many slices of cold meat as he could hold, and surreptitiously deposited them into his trousers pocket.

"They are," whispered the barkeep, "members of the Autonomie Club up on Windmill Street. Anarchists, all three of them."

"What, in heaven's name," I demanded, "are they doing here?"

"Other than stealing tomorrow's lunch, it is hard to tell. We overhear some of them saying that they hate the dancers because they are tools of the Czar, and he is using them to burnish his image abroad. Others, particularly the younger fellows, seem to think they can recruit new members. They foolishly believe that because a dancer has an independent spirit when it comes to the arts or personal morality, they will also lean toward revolutionary politics."

"And do they?" I asked.

"Perhaps. Mind you, one of the leaders of the anarchists who used to live in London referred to such artists as *useful idiots*. Unfortunately for those starving revolutionaries, the dancers are not here tonight."

I watched as one of the anarchists, his pockets now bulging, sidled up to an attractive young woman. He leaned his head toward her ear and appeared to be saying something. She responded by giving him a look that could have frozen a volcano and walked away.

The barkeep was struggling to repress his laughter. "Better luck next time, Igor," he muttered.

"Why," I asked, "does the hotel allow mashers like that to enter the premises?"

"The fellow in charge, that Diaghilev chap, says we must not create a fuss and throw them out. Such an incident would then become the story in the Press the following day instead of the opening of the ballet. So as long as they do not start shouting their slogans, we ignore them. And they know that the Okhrana fellow will send his thugs to give them a thorough beating if they embarrass Mother Russia. Mind you, we do not trust any of them. But all I can do is keep the bottles of vodka under the table where they cannot be pilfered by either party."

As the crowd began to thin, Countess Betsy returned to us, beaming like the cat who swallowed the canary.

"*Yolki*, Sherlock, do I have a story? *Da*, what a story I have. It is juicier than even I could have imagined and, I assure you, my imagination is not lacking in degeneracy."

"We are all attention," said Holmes.

"Oh my. Where to start? Nijinsky. *Da*, I start with Nijinsky. Everyone here calls him "our Vatsa." He was a poor boy from Kiev but an exceptional dancer, and so, when he is seventeen years old, he is made a member of the Imperial Ballet in St. Petersburg. What does he find there? He finds that there are rich, older men who, to use their words, "adopt" pretty boys from the ballet. No less than Prince Lvov adopts Vaslav. The Prince looks after Vaslav every day, and the boy looks after the prince every night, if you know what I mean. The Prince passes off Vaslav to his friend, Serge Diaghilev, and Serge adopts Vaslav. He recruits him away from the Imperial Ballet and into *Les Ballets Russes* and makes him the most famous male dancer in the world. He can leap and show passion with his body like no other man has ever done on the stage. Serge tells Vaslav to be a choreographer. So Vaslav Nijinsky creates *The Faun* and *The Rite of Spring*. Some say these ballets are brilliant, the work of a genius. Others that they are terrible, the work of a depraved madman.

"Serge is worried about the reaction of audiences, so he takes the choreographer job away from Nijinsky and gives it back to Fokine. Our Vaslav is upset. The whole *Ballets Russes* company goes on tour this past summer to South America. Serge does not go with them because some gypsy told him that he will die on the water, so Serge does not like long boat trips. But this young woman, the one you saw attached to Nijinsky, Miss Romola de Pulszky, does go along. She is in love, utterly besotted with Nijinsky. She adores him. She pesters him all the way to Brazil and convinces him that he is in love with her even though they have no language in common. In Rio, they buy engagement rings. In Buenos Aires, they find a church, San Miguel Arcangel, and they get married. Our Vaslav is happy.

"When Serge finds out, he is not happy. He does not like to lose his pretty boy. Now there is a rumor that he will fire Nijinsky. Throw him out of *Les Ballets Russes*. The whole company hears this rumor. They are in turmoil. They will still perform here in London because many tickets have already been sold, and Nijinsky will be on the stage. But after that, who knows? The company is like a swan. Gliding smoothly across the water, but beneath, the feet are going crazy.

"Now, I ask you, my dear Sherlock, is not that a good story? What else do you want to know?"

Chapter Five

Diaghilev Comes at Midnight

olmes and I listened, , wide-eyed and fascinated.

"Indeed, my dear Countess," said Holmes, "a very good story. All is not well in the land of Russian ballet dancers, it seems. I now have several other avenues of inquiry to make."

Our gala evening ended. The two of us returned to Baker Street and a late-evening glass of port.

"Any thoughts or insights, my friend?" said Holmes to me after I had lit the hearth and stretched out in my customary padded chair. I took a long slow sip of Port as I mentally prepared my considered response. I was about to commence my dissertation when I was interrupted by a loud ringing of the bell on Baker Street, followed by a forceful banging on the door.

"Merciful heavens," I said. "it is almost midnight. Who in the world could be coming at this hour?"

Holmes merely shrugged. I rose and, Mrs. Hudson having long retired for the night, descended the stairs and opened the door. Mr. Serge Diaghilev rudely pushed past me was a curt *"Dobryy vecher"* and began climbing the stairs. I followed him.

He positioned himself in the center of the room and looked directly at Holmes.

"Mr. Holmes, I thank you for coming this evening to reception for *Les Ballets Russes*. I am most grateful. I am never forget your kindness."

"And I," said Holmes, "will never believe that you have come here at this hour merely to express your gratitude."

"Ah. You are very smart man, Mr. Holmes. Yes. I am here because I need help from you."

"Then kindly be seated and state your case, preferably with a minimum of dramatic flourishes."

It was difficult to look at the man seated on the sofa and think that just two hours earlier, he was smiling and joking with his adoring fans and sycophants at the Savoy. Mr. Serge Diaghilev now appeared deeply distressed.

"Forgive me, Mr. Holmes, when we met earlier for not saying to you everything I should have."

"Agreed. Please get on with what should have said."

"My company ... my dancers ... my *children* ... we have big trouble come upon us."

"Go on."

"Where to start? My company, my *Ballets Russes* is tearing apart. How does this happen? It starts with Nijinsky. Vaslav I discover in St. Petersburg. He is brilliant dancer. Genius. I invite him to join my *Ballet Russes*. I make him famous. He is now most famous man dancer in entire world. I make him choreographer. He creates new ballets. He is genius but very modern. Too modern for audiences. We argue. I give next assignment for choreographer not to Nijinsky but back to Fokine. Vaslav is hurt. We argue. We cannot reconcile. He is dancer, so very ... how you say? ... very passionate. He say to me that he will quit *Ballets Russe*s because of differences. Now whole company is in turmoil. Someone is trying to steal company from me ..."

Holmes quickly stood up and pointed a finger at Diaghilev.

"Get out!" he ordered. "Get out of here this minute and do not dare to come back!"

Diaghilev looked shocked. "Mr. Holmes ..."

"You heard me. Get out of here!"

"Why you say me this?"

"I have no use whatsoever for men who tell me lies to my face. The entire West End knows that you have dismissed Nijinsky because he married and now prefers to spend his nights in his wife's bed, not yours. What you just told me was a pack of lies. Now get out."

Diaghilev remained seated on the sofa. He raised both hands, palms facing Holmes.

"I am sorry, Mr. Holmes. I am sorry ..."

"I have no use for your apology. I will not deal with liars. Now leave."

"Mr. Holmes, I beg you. Two of my children are murdered. I come here because another one of them, just a child, her life is in danger. She will also be murdered. You must help. I will tell truth and only truth. I promise."

His utterance demanded Holmes's attention, and he sat down and crossed his arms across his chest.

"Very well. State your case. And if you lie to me again, I will throw you down the stairs. Is that understood?"

"*Da*. I understand. You are right, sir. I tell Nijinsky to leave *Ballets Russes*. This upsets whole company. Someone, I do not know who, someone sends messages to my dancers saying that they are invited to join new company. Nijinsky will come with them they are told. New company will give better pay. They are told, forget Diaghilev and come to new company. But must be kept secret from Diaghilev. Two dancers, Tatiana and Luka. They are loyal to me. They love me. I introduce them to each other and they become lovers and so they love me. They come to me and say me about this attempt to steal my company. I say them, please, be my spies. Pretend to want to join new company and report back to me. They agree. Next thing ... next thing, they are murdered. Whoever does this knows they are

49

spies. I am sorry, I should have said you this before. Because they are loyal to me and I make them spies, now they are dead."

He stopped, closed his eyes, and clenched his fists and took several deep breaths. Then he continued.

"They are not only dancers who come to me. Also comes Veronika Vinokurova. She is mere child. Only has sixteen years. She is niece, daughter of my brother in Novgorod. On mother's side, has important relatives. I promise my brother and his wife I protect their daughter. She joins company and is good dancer. Plays swan, or maybe servant, or maybe child. She has promise. But she is my niece and loyal to her uncle. She also comes me and says me what she overhears about secret invitation to join new company. I also ask her to be spy. She agrees. Now I fear whoever found out Tanya and Lukasha and killed them also knows Veronika is spy and will kill her. Please, Mr. Holmes. I am beg you. You must help me find killers and protect her."

For several moments, Holmes said nothing. He was looking at our visitor very intently. I was reasonably sure that Mr. Diaghilev was telling the truth now, and I assumed Holmes thought the same.

"Why," asked Holmes, "have you come to me? Why have you not gone to Scotland Yard?"

"If necessary ... if you not help me, I go to Scotland Yard. But if I go and say all to them, they make order that all remaining shows in London be canceled and *Ballet Russes* sent back to Paris. Then *Ballets Russes* is bankrupt. Creditors seize everything. There is no performance in Paris. We are over.

Everyone is ruined and goes back to Russia. Whoever killed Tatiana and Luka is never caught. Whoever killed them gets away with murder and can now form new company. I do not want this. I need help of Sherlock Holmes."

"Arresting murderers," said Holmes, "is a prospect that attracts me. Preventing another murder of an innocent young person compels me. Saving your company from bankruptcy is your concern, not mine. Besides which, I am informed that *Ballets Russes* is already bankrupt. Is that not true?"

"*Nyet*. Not at all. We are in debt. *Da*. But bankrupt? *Nyet*. Is opposite. We are sold out all this week in London. We are sell out until Christmas in Paris at Opéra. We lose money on tour of South America because Czar tell Diaghilev that we must take Russian culture to world and we lose money. But now we are most famous ballet in world and we are … how you say? … a gold mine. Everywhere we are sell out to big houses. By end of London we pay off all debts and in profit. *Ochen' vygodno*! Why you think someone want to steal *Ballets Russes* from me? Is not any good if bankrupt. Only worth stealing and murder if profitable."

"How much profit?" asked Holmes.

"*Mnogo*. We go to Paris. We double price for ticket. Accountant and banker agree that by Christmas we have half million French franc. We go to America; we make ticket three maybe four times. They agree we have one hundred thousand dollar profit every month. Now you see why someone want to steal and murder."

"Ah," mused Holmes. "That does cast things in a different light. Much more interesting. Yes, Mr. Diaghilev, your case is of interest to me."

"*Spasibo,* Mr. Holmes. I pay you well. Very big money if you find murderer and protect my niece."

"You will pay me nothing," said Holmes. "I have already been consulted on this case by Scotland Yard. They are my client. I cannot serve two masters. Therefore, I cannot also work for you. If you have any further information about your case that would be useful to me, kindly furnish it now."

The impresario produced a photo of his niece. She looked no more than fourteen years old and all innocence. He had a full list of the members of his company and had marked off those who he suspected might be willing to abandon him and join a competing enterprise. He also had a complete schedule of all upcoming performances both in London and on the Continent. Holmes took these from him and asked many questions. I furiously scribbled down his answers. By one o'clock in the morning, I had tired, and Diaghilev seemed exhausted. Holmes was utterly awake and alive. Our visitor departed, leaving Holmes and me to one final glass of port.

He looked over at me with a friendly smile.

"My dear doctor, I fear I must impose on your generous spirit."

"Yes?"

"My knowledge of the universe of dance is severely limited. In order to gain useful insights into this case, I must acquire far more expertise than I now have and do so rather quickly."

"Yes?"

"Beginning at opening hours tomorrow morning, I shall present myself to the desk of the library of the British Museum and request a cartload of books, ancient and modern, on dance and ballet. Therefore, I must ask a favor of you."

"Yes?"

"Would it be possible for you to rearrange your schedule and provide a close shadow to this Miss Veronika and see that she comes to no harm during the course of this week? She is living, as you just heard from Mr. Diaghilev, in a rooming house in the West End. Given that she keeps the hours of the theater crowd, it is highly unlikely that she will rise any time before noon, but between that time and her showing up at the stage door of the Royal Opera Theatre, she could wander anywhere in London. She will need to be closely followed and kept from harm. Might I beseech you to take on that task."

"Yes," I said. "Of course, I will."

"It may be deadly boring and utterly meaningless."

"That is what a book and a notepad are for," I said.

Chapter Six

I am Not That Old

The following day was a Monday. I rose early and hastened to my medical office and made arrangements for my colleagues to cover appointments with patients whose ailments were serious and to postpone those—the majority of them—whose complaints varied between hypochondria and malingering. By eleven, I was seated at a table by the front window of a café on Mercer Street, immediately across from the rooming house in which Miss Veronika Vinokurova was residing during her week in London. I had brought with me a newly purchased copy of the latest novel by a promising young writer, a Mr. David Lawrence. It was titled *Sons and Lovers,* and the reviews had been mixed. Some critics complained that it was indecent whilst others praised its modernity and brilliance. Just in case, I wrapped it in the paper jacket of an older novel, *Paul Clifford,* which might lead to questions as to my literary maturity but assuredly not to rumors about my seeking sensuous titillation in my now advancing years.

By noon, not a single soul had emerged from the rooming house, and I began to wonder if the location we had been given was correct. But then a pair of young women appeared, followed by three more sets of twos and threes, but none of them looked at all like the Miss Veronika I had been instructed to follow. At twenty past noon, a group of six girls appeared all laughing gayly as if they had just been let out of school. Miss Veronika was a member of the pack, and I quickly thanked the café owner and began to follow them. All of them were young and exceptionally beautiful, and I knew that under no circumstances could I be seen to be following them, as a gentleman of my vintage being so observed would arouse far more unkind speculation than being caught reading a racy novel.

The squad of them were chattering loudly in Russian and giggling incessantly, so much so that I felt a pang of profound sympathy for the school teachers who had to endure such an age every day. They walked up Mercer, turned left on Earlham, and then left again on Shaftsbury Avenue. Within ten minutes, they were standing by the fountain in Piccadilly Circus and soon could be seen chatting in English and smiling coyly in the company of some lads dressed in the blazers of King's College. I could see that my Russian ballerina was quite comfortable and confident in the language of flirtation. Most likely, they could do the same in French. Some fifteen minutes of smiles, admiring looks, and charming laughter passed before the entire lot of boys and girls departed Piccadilly and walked en masse toward Leicester Square. Just past the Prince of Wales Theatre, they entered a select restaurant in which, I was quite certain, the bewitched students would soon be parted from their monthly allowances.

I stood across the street and read a copy of the *Times* and constantly checked my watch so as to give the look of a gentleman who was waiting for a tardy friend. An hour later, the group emerged, and I was quite shocked on seeing the young women plant friendly kisses on both cheeks of the lads before sending them back to their afternoon classes. I concluded, much to my dismay, that the morality of convenience, so notorious amongst the leading dancers and other artists of this age had been passed down all too quickly to this unchaperoned troupe of girls. Had I more time, I might have reflected on that thought, but they set off quickly in the direction of Regent Street, and once they were finished with their window shopping, they descended on the select stores of Bond Street. They did not dare venture into any of those retail establishments but soon found their way into Fortnum and Mason.

For two full hours, they wandered the departments of the great store, picking up and putting down endless articles of clothing, hats, gloves and the like. I watched from a distance with my newspaper in hand. I was approached by several shop-ladies asking if I needed assistance. I smiled and replied with the universal response of gentlemen trapped in such a situation.

"I am waiting for my wife," I told them, accompanied by a weary sigh. They gave a well-practiced word of solace and left me alone.

Finally, the young women departed F & M. As I exited the store and stepped back on to the pavement, I noticed a large maroon-colored motor car parked across the street. I had seen the same car parked not far from the door of the select restaurant where the girls had enjoyed their lunch. It was in all likelihood a coincidence—those who patronize fine restaurants also shop in expensive stores—but I made a note of its registration number all the same.

Several stops were made along the way at food carts and pavement merchants, all accompanied by shrieks and giggles. At one point during the slow meander back to the rooming house, it struck me that these dancers were running late for their call for tonight's performance, but then I remembered that Monday is a dark night throughout almost all of the West End. They could wander until midnight, and I would still have to follow them, a prospect that I found too exhausting to think about.

Fortunately, by seven o'clock, they had returned to Mercer Street, and I returned to my seat in the café opposite the door of the rooming house. To my great relief, they did not re-emerge that evening.

The following morning, I returned to my table at the same café and waited. Again, sometime after eleven o'clock, twos and threes of young Russian dancers came out of the rooming house door and made their way up Mercer Street. However, it was eleven-thirty before Miss Veronika Vinokurova emerged. She was very smartly dressed and made up and was, even to an aging eye as mine, quite the beauty. To my surprise, she did not walk north toward Shaftsbury, but south toward the Strand. She was walking quickly and even seemed to have a lively spring in her step. Then she began to run, interrupted with an occasional skip. Had I been a twenty-year-old and not well past sixty, I might have been able to keep up with her. Wisely, I stopped a cab that was going in the same direction.

Cab drivers are understandably loath to assist a man of mature years in the pursuit of a pretty girl who is more than forty years younger.

"Driver," I said as I hopped into his cab. "My name is Dr. John Watson. I write the stories about Sherlock Holmes? Are you familiar with them?"

"Well, of course, I am, Guv'nor. Read every one of them. Honor to have you in my cab, but I would have given you a good ride even if you was a nobody."

"I am sure you would, sir. I identified myself so that you could help Sherlock Holmes and me prevent a terrible crime. Do you see a young woman in a black cape up ahead on the right? She's walking quickly. See who I mean?"

"Right. I sees her, doctor. What are we to do with her?"

"Please," I said. "Just keep up with her and do not let her get out of sight. Keep close. Can you do that?"

"Sure and I can. As long as it's for Sherlock Holmes, it will be no trouble at all."

He was as good as his word. Miss Veronika zigged and zagged her way south until she was skipping down Southampton Street on her way to the Strand. Then I saw her wave. At the corner, a man waved back. As we drew closer, I could see that it was one of the young men from King's who had been with the group for lunch yesterday. I relaxed. Obviously, they had been attracted to each other and had made a plan to meet again today. Possibly, they were going for an elegant lunch at the Savoy. I could not fault the young man for his taste in either dining establishments or lovely young ballerinas. He was, after all, a university lad.

I watched and smiled as he greeted her, reaching for her hand and bowing gallantly. I could not see her face, but he was all smiles and laughter. It had all the trappings of a blossoming affair of young love and rather brought a warm feeling to my heart. I was about to tell the driver that he could take me back to Baker Street and then decided not to.

A large maroon motor car pulled up along the Strand just behind the young man. It stopped. Suddenly a thick thuggish-looking fellow jumped out. In two steps, he was standing behind the lad and gave him a hard sucker punch to the side of his head. He dropped sideways, almost falling into the traffic turning from Southampton on to the Strand. Then he lunged forward toward Veronkia. She turned to run, but it was too late. He had his arms around her, lifted her off the ground, and moved rapidly back into the motor car. The car took off straight away and sped along the Strand.

"After him!" I shouted to the driver. At the corner, I flung the door open and shouted to the student who was staggering back to his feet.

"Get in!" I screamed at him. "She is in danger!"

He stared at me for a split second and then took two running steps and dove into the car through the open door.

"Can you catch them!?" I shouted to the driver.

"Just you hold on there Dr. Watson, we'll be on him in no time."

The young fellow had managed to get his body off the floor and up on to the seat of the cab beside me. He looked at me, eyes wide.

"Dr. Watson? *The* Dr. Watson who helps Sherlock Holmes?"

"Yes. Now, listen and listen carefully. Veronika was grabbed and dragged into that maroon car up ahead. See it. They likely do not know that we are following them. When they stop in traffic, we both get out. Veronika will still be on the left side, as that was the way she was dragged into the car. The thug will be on the right. When I say *go*, we both fly out of the car and run up to that one and open doors on both sides. You go to the left. Grab the thug by the hair and go for his eyes. Gouge, hard. No mercy. I will go to the right and pull Veronika out. Do you understand?"

"Uh ... yes. Yes, sir. But why would anybody try to kidnap her?"

"Questions later, young man. Get ready to move."

The car we were following had moved east along the Strand, past the Savoy, and into the turn lane that would take it over Waterloo bridge. It stopped at the intersection, waiting for a break in the oncoming traffic. We were still several cars behind, but I estimated we had a good fifteen seconds to make our move.

"Now!" I shouted.

I leapt out the left side, and my newly acquired accomplice did the same on the right. He was faster on his feet than I was and, in a flash, was at the target, had the door open, and had the thug's head most of the way out of the car whilst driving his fingers into his eyes. I opened the other door, leaned in, and wrapped my arms around the girl's legs and pulled.

Our monster was not about to give up easily. He kept his one arm locked around Veronika's neck whilst defending his eyes and fending off his attacker with the other. We had only a few more seconds before traffic would clear and the car would start moving.

Then Veronika took action.

She turned her head to the side, forced her mouth forward along a burly arm, and sunk her teeth deep into his thumb joint. The blood spurted from his hand across Veronika's mouth as he screamed with pain. By instinct, he pulled his hand back, releasing his grip on her neck. I pulled hard on her legs and, using my own, braced against the running board to give me leverage. She came sliding out, and the two of us ended up in a tangled heap on the road.

The maroon car roared off through the intersection, turned and raced toward the open expanse of Waterloo Bridge.

The ballerina sprang to her feet, and I soon felt multiple sets of hands on my arms, lifting me up off the roadway and partly leading, partly carrying me back to the pavement. Suddenly, I had become the victim, and these two absurdly fit young people, and my cab driver were intent on rescuing me.

"The Savoy is just ahead. We can take him in there," said the lad. He paid the driver, and then he and Veronika half-carried me along the pavement to the door of the Savoy.

Once through the door, he shouted at the bellboy.

"Oscar, some help here, please."

The uniformed bellboy shouted at one of the maids who ran over to us, bearing the tray of damp scented towels that the hotel had on hand for greeting weary guests. The maid offered one straight away to Veronika, whose mouth and chin were covered with blood.

"No!" she shouted. "It is not me. It is this poor old man. Help him!"

By now, I was back on my feet and, having disentangled from the helpful hands and arms of my rescuers, I reasserted my dignity.

"Please. Enough," I said. "Kindly, follow me through to the bar. We need to have a few words." I began moving immediately toward the bar before either of the two of them or the now three bellboys could grab on to my arms and steer me as if I were a common drunk.

I led them to a table in the hotel bar. A waiter in starched black and white appeared immediately at our table.

"Good morning, Master Stapleton-Cotton. Lovely to see you again," he said to the student. "Some refreshment? Perhaps something warm on a November morning?"

"Thank you, Ronnie," said the lad, whose name I now knew. "Dr. John Watson, the best-selling writer in all of England, and a frightfully brave man as well, is my guest. What will you have, Doctor?"

"Just a brandy," I said.

"Would Hennessey be acceptable, sir?" asked the waiter.

Before I could reply and opine that I was not in the habit of paying a month's wage for a snifter of brandy, my Viscount-to-be interrupted.

"An excellent suggestion, Ronnie. And the young lady would likely enjoy a chilled glass of fruit juice."

"*Nyet*," came the immediate reply from Veronika. "*Molodaya ledi khotela by vodki na l'du.*" She smiled coyly at the waiter.

"*Bezuslovno,*" replied Ronnie with a pleasant laugh. "Coming up right away, miss."

"Forgive me," said the young man, "for failing to introduce myself properly. Please, Doctor, ignore my last name and just call me Tom. And you appear to already know who this young lady is. I do not wish to be rude, but you really must tell us what this was all about. It is not every day that some thug knocks my block off, and kidnaps the girl I am with, only to be rescued by the partner of Sherlock Holmes."

"Sherlock Holmes?" gasped Miss Veronika. "The man who is famous detective?"

"Yes, my dear. And this wonderful gentleman is the one who records all of his adventures. This is Doctor Watson, the famous writer."

"*Bozhe moy*. Then please tell me why it is someone grabs me and tries to kidnap me, and what does Mr. Sherlock Holmes have to do with any of this?"

I took a small sip on my over-priced brandy and looked solemnly at one then the other.

"I am of the opinion that both of you are people of sterling character, and I have to demand that whatever I tell you must never leave this room. Will you agree to that?"

"What does he mean?" Veronika demanded of Tom.

"He means that we have to keep it a secret."

"*Da*. I can do that."

"You as well?" I demanded of Tom.

"Sure. I can keep a secret. This is getting to be quite the jolly adventure, I must say."

"Very well," I said. "Miss Veronika Vinokurova, an attempt was made to kidnap you because some party has learned that you agreed to work as a spy for your Uncle Serge."

"My golly!" blustered Tom. "You're a spy. Wow. Isn't that just bang up the elephant. The boys at King's will be in a stitch when I tell them that you're a spy."

"No, Tom," I said quite sharply. "They will not be because they will never know. You may never say anything to them. If you do, Miss Veronika's life could be in danger."

"Oh. Yes. Sorry. I will keep it a secret. I promise."

"That's better," I said. "Your uncle knows that someone is trying to take *Les Ballets Russes* away from him, and whoever is trying to do so is prepared to do very evil deeds to get what he wants."

"Like kidnap people?" asked Tom.

"Or worse."

"Is it so?" asked Tom, incredulous. "Here I thought these music hall folks were all nanty narkers."

"We are not music hall," snapped Miss Veronika. "We are artists. If you think I am music hall girl, you leave right now."

There was a spark of fire in her eye. Whilst she gave the nonplussed Tom a hard look, I looked closely at her. On her head, she had perfectly arranged golden blonde hair. Her face was pale but without a single blemish. Her eyes were set wide and had a faint hint of the oriental to them. She was breathtakingly beautiful. Tom was struggling for words.

"Oh no, no, I know you are an artist, my dear. Of course, you are. It's just that ... well ... the people in the business of looking after our theaters, both artistic and vulgar, always seemed like a jocular lot. That's what I meant."

She seemed mollified and continued.

"Your uncle ..."

"Her uncle?" interrupted Tom. "Who is your uncle?"

"My uncle is Serge Diaghilev."

"The impresario?" asked Tom. "The chap behind all those ballet shows?"

"*Da*. He is my uncle. My mother is twenty-third cousin to Czar. What of it?"

"Your Uncle Serge," I said, "has asked Sherlock Holmes to investigate and find out who is behind the attempt to take the company away from him."

"Really?" asked Tom. "Why would anyone want to do that? Doesn't everybody love him?"

"*Nyet*," said the young woman. "He is difficult man to work with. He thinks that universe should revolve around him. He shouts at dancers. He insults them. He makes them feel bad. Then he does not give wages on time. He is brother to my father, so I must stay with him. He is family. But many are unhappy with him, especially after we learn he will get rid of Nijinsky."

"No," exclaimed Tom. "he can't do that. That Nijinsky chap is the best there is. They say he electrifies that stage, *the whole theater* when he dances. Or ... or maybe it's Nijinsky that's behind trying to break up the company. Maybe that's who it is."

"*Nyet. Ne stat' glupym*. Nijinsky is unbelievable dancer. We are all in awe of him. As dancer, we worship him. But he is

... how do you say ... dumb bell. Try to talk to him is like talking to dog. He hears nobody but himself. Maybe now his wife. Maybe in the past, he listened to Diaghilev. Not now. No one will ever leave *Les Ballets Russes* and work for Vaslav. It would be disaster."

"If not Nijinsky," I asked. "who could it be?"

"No one knows," she said. "There is meeting planned sometime, but I have not been invited. They know that Diaghilev is my uncle and that I cannot leave him. I say to him that I will not be very good spy because I will never know anything because I am his niece."

Without revealing anything about the two murdered dancers, I asked her some questions and made oblique references to the score and mysterious page of numbers. She knew the score, but that was all. I concluded that I would get no more useful information from Miss Veronika but that her safety was still an issue.

"Tom," I said. "You need to stay with Veronika for the rest of the afternoon. I suggest you remain here at the Savoy. No one is likely to try to kidnap her again as long as she is here. Then, at six-thirty, you need to have a hotel car and driver take both of you to the stage door of the Royal Opera House and escort her into the green room. What you do after that is up to you, but I recommend that you find a ticket somehow and enjoy the evening. Can you do all that, young man?"

"I would be happy to, of course, but I have some duties at school."

"You may tell them that you have been requested by Sherlock Holmes to assist in a case. If they doubt your word, you may have them call me at this number." I handed him my card.

"Gosh. Yesterday morning, I was complaining about how dull my life as a student had become now that we were in late November. Guess I cannot do that anymore. You can count on me, Dr. Watson."

I bid the lovely young couple adieu, thinking that they were already starting to look longingly at each other. Miss Veronika would be safe in the care of Thomas Stapleton-Cotton, and I could put in a couple of hours of work. I took a cab back to my medical practice.

Chapter Seven

A Magnificent Swan and a Perverse Faun

The afternoon passed in a desultory manner as I tended to the unending whinges and complaints of the English populace. At five o'clock, I said goodbye to the last old fellow and walked the few blocks back to Baker Street. Holmes was sitting by the hearth, pipe in mouth, and surrounded by small piles of books and manuscripts that bore the markings of the library in the British Museum.

"Oh, hello, Watson. I have asked Mrs. Hudson to prepare an early supper. That will give us time to dress and get to the theater well before curtain time."

I agreed and then asked, "Any insights into the current case?"

"If by that you mean that I am quickly deducing that every party involved cannot be trusted to tell the truth, then, yes. I am holding out some hope for the innocence of the young dancers, but beyond that, I fear that cynicism may overwhelm me."

"Very well, Holmes. On a more cheerful note, are you becoming an expert in matters pertaining to ballet?"

He offered a small smile to that one. "As you know, Watson, my turn to an interest in the arts has been in my veins, thanks perhaps to my grandmother, the sister of Vernet. Unfortunately, art in the blood took the strange form of leaving me ignorant of this exquisite and magnificent form of creative expression."

"You are not alone," I said. "For the past century, all of England appears to have believed that the highest form of dance consisted in making sure that a lady did not accept two invitations to the same foxtrot."

Holmes chuckled. "Yes, and during that time, to our further chagrin, the classical ballet has been sequestered in all places, Mother Russia. All those years, we of the ruling class of the world wrote off the Slavs as no more than a mass of serfs dominated by a French-speaking cabal of Czars and Czarinas and their endless cousins."

"Are you," I asked, "learning anything of use to the case of *our* Russian ballet dancers?"

"All newly acquired knowledge is useful, my friend. But no, nothing has emerged that is immediately applicable. However, I confess to having spent several profoundly satisfying and enjoyable hours in my pursuit, which seems terribly unfair to you when I consider that you have done no more than follow a coterie of mindless debutantes through the shops."

"In truth," I responded, feeling somewhat triumphant, "my day was not in the least boring. I prevented a kidnapping and quite possibly another horrible murder, with some help, of course. I would never wish to take the entire credit."

That got his attention. Down went the scholarly study of the *pas de deux*, and he demanded a full account, which, after feigning reluctance and protesting that I did not wish to interrupt his profoundly satisfying studies, I gave. By the end of my account, my old friend was utterly beaming at me.

"Well done, old fellow," he chortled. "Well done, indeed. So good to see that your military training has not abandoned you, and you still seize the moment and rush toward the cannon's roar. Well done. Now, did you happen to get a description of the thug or the driver?"

"And a registration number for the car?" I chided.

"Yes, yes. Of course."

"The number, I have. As to the thug, he was young but a thick, swarthy fellow, needing a change of clothes and a shave, but rather like a hundred of those blokes who could be found in an hour in the East End."

"Yes, yes. But did he have any distinguishing marks?"

"He has," I said after a moment of reflection, "a very sore thumb. It is quite likely to stick out, if I may say so, rather like ... a sore thumb."

Holmes smiled at my attempt at wit. "Very true, my dear chap. I shall let loose the latest band of my Irregulars and will likely have a report back by this time tomorrow. But now I hear our Mrs. Hudson approaching with what promises to be our supper. Let us enjoy it, and then we shall be on our way to the West End."

We arrived in ample time at the Royal Opera House. The theater had a well-earned reputation for pulling up the drawbridge and shutting its doors at one minute before curtain time, banishing late-comers to the bar until the first intermission. As the first item on the program for the evening was the twelve-minute *Après midi d'un faune*, we would have missed the entire performance had we been tardy. A split second before the doors closed, Countess Betsy appeared and trod across a half a row of feet that were foolishly not pulled back and then took her seat beside us. I am sure she was about to deliver a loud soliloquy and would have had Holmes not silenced her with and brusque "Sssh." The three of us sat back and prepared to enjoy the performance.

The ballet was shocking.

Nijinsky played the role of a male faun waking from his slumber to find a cluster of desirable barefooted nymphs moving about in an irresistibly erotic manner. He chases them about the stage, and the specific desire of his affections escapes his grasp, leaving her scarf behind. The ballet concludes with his performing an act which decency does not allow me to name but may be understood if I refer to the jibe, common amongst schoolboys, of shouting the augmented biblical instruction to "Go forth and multiply ... *by yourself!*"

When the curtain closed, there was a moment of stunned silence, and then a well-diamonded woman in one of the select boxes leapt to her feet and began applauding enthusiastically. She was followed by several other women in the audience who, I suspect, also made generous donations to the women's suffrage cause. Soon, half of the audience was cheering and clapping while the non-applauding members sat in silence, cowed by the fear of being labeled as degenerate aesthetes. A closer look at the woman who led the response revealed that she was none other Mrs. Elsie Cubitt.

During the brief twelve minutes of the performance, my eyes had been glued to the stage. It was as if the Portland vase had come to life. Holmes, on the other hand, had a copy of the Debussy score open in his lap and kept moving his gaze from the score to the stage and back again. At the final curtain, he had folded up the score and shook his head.

"We may as well join the unruly mob in the bar for the first intermission," he said as he rose from his seat and began to move in that direction. Countess Betsy and I followed.

"Countess," said Holmes, after we had been served our first glass of Champagne, "kindly continue to do the work you do so brilliantly. Please go and chat and listen and report back to me at the next intermission. Thank you, my dear."

She gave Holmes a smug grin and then disengaged herself from the bar and disappeared into the chattering barons and earls and *nouveaux riches.*

The second performance of the evening, *Swan Lake,* was a rapturous joy to watch. The roles of both the beautiful and innocent Odette and the treacherous Odile were danced by Mathilde Kschessinska, and Vaslav Nijinsky danced as Siegfried. Many times, after a spectacular dance—the *pas des quatre danse des petits cygnes* or the *pas de deux*—the dancers had to hold their positions whilst the audience erupted into spontaneous applause. And all of us, even Holmes, were swept into clapping along with the music as Odile danced the electrifying feat that only a Russian ballerina could deliver, the perfectly executed thirty-two continuous fouettés.

By the end of the performance, I could hear the muffled sobs of some of the ladies in the audience as Odette lay dying in her lover's arms, and the two of them disappeared beneath the waves. The curtain fell, and the entire house sprang to its feet in a thunderous ovation. The Countess and I were on our feet, clapping furiously and shouting. Holmes was not.

His eyes were closed, and his hands were beneath his chin with his fingertips pressed together. He was slowly shaking his head.

"Let us go," he said, once the final bows had been taken. "There is nothing else to be gained here."

We bade the Countess good night and hailed a cab from the long line of them that were strung out along Bow Street. As I climbed in, I happened to catch a glance of the crowd of devotees huddled around the stage door. Master Tom of King's College was standing there, shivering, but clutching a bouquet of roses. I smiled inwardly. My faith in the much-maligned student generation was restored.

Holmes climbed in after me and quickly slouched into the corner of the back seat, tucking his chin into his chest and pulling his hat down. I attempted to make conversation and had only managed to get a few words out when he interrupted me.

"You have a grand gift of silence, Watson. Please be so kind as to exercise it."

Which I did.

And I stayed that way until we were back inside the hallowed cloister of 221B. I poured each of us a glass of port and then decided it was time to poke the bear.

"Am I to remain silent?" I asked. "Or is Mr. Sherlock Holmes now in the mood for civil conversation?"

He did not answer my question. Instead, he took a sip of his port and spread a musical score out on the table.

"The two dancers who were murdered had a copy of *this* score and *this* list of numbers. You reported to me that Miss Veronika heard that some meeting was planned of the potential defectors to which she was clearly *not* invited and that she was not familiar with these cryptic numbers. Therefore, it is possible that some sort of message lies therein, but I can make no sense of it."

"The first line ..." I started to say.

"Oh, yes, Watson. The first line is easy. It states a specific date and time. *C.G. 28 – 11 – 11.00.* That must refer to the twenty-eighth day of the month of November—that would be this Friday—at eleven o'clock in the morning. The lines of numbers that follow are a complete blank. And I have no insight into the possible meaning of *C.G.* Do you?"

I pondered his question for a moment. "Might it be the location of a meeting? Covent Garden, for example. That would be within easy reach of whoever was invited. They are all residing in the West End."

Holmes nodded his head slowly and then replied. "That is good thinking, my friend. It makes some sense. Thank you. But if the first line gives the date, time, and location of the meeting, what is the purpose of the remaining dozen lines of numbers? So, no. It cannot be that straightforward. The cipher must in some way be tied to this score. And it must be something that a member, *any* member of the company would be able to see and solve. Yet to us, it is as clear as mud."

It was too much for me at that hour of night. I finished my port, bade my friend a good night, and went to bed. I would not have been surprised had I wakened seven hours later to find him still in his chair.

Chapter Eight

Holmes Fails to Solve the Code

olmes was not sitting in his chair come morning. In fact, he was not in the house at all. I had no idea when he departed, but it must have been before I rose at seven o'clock. Mrs. Hudson delivered a nourishing breakfast, which I enjoyed whilst reading the morning newspapers. The reviews of the performance at the Royal Opera House spanned critical opinion from the sublime to the ridiculous. All of the papers gave glowing praise to *Swan Lake*, but the opinions expressed of *The Faun* were nowhere near as consensual. The *Times* acknowledged that it was "innovative and *avant-garde*" but cautioned that families intending to bring their children to see Thursday's performance of *The Nutcracker* were advised to arrive after the short first ballet if they wished to avoid awkward explanations concerning the unseemly actions of the Faun and the nymph's scarf. The *Daily Mirror* and the *Evening Star*, wishing to retain their pretense of modernity, gave their stamp of approval, noting that the Victorian Age was now well in the past. The *Daily Telegraph* declared the piece to be utterly degenerate, catering to man's basest instincts and bemoaned the diminishing of the power of the office of the Lord Chamberlain, noting that under the Theatres Act of 1853, the current holder of the office, the Lord Sandhurst, still retained the power to banish a production if "it is fitting for the preservation of good manners, decorum or of the public peace so to do."

I was about to depart in order to spend another day serving as the guardian angel to Miss Veronika Vinokurova when a delivery boy brought a note. It was printed on a very fine stock of paper, addressed to me, and bore the return insignia of a house in Mayfair. It ran:

My dear Doctor Watson:
Words cannot express my gratitude to you for your prompt and courageous actions yesterday as you rescued such a beautiful, brilliant, and spirited young woman, Miss Veronika Vinokurova, from certain peril. Whilst I

assure you that I have repeatedly given all credit to you, she insists on treating me as her hero and bestowing such affection upon me as might be the stuff that dreams are made of.

I fear that she may still be in danger and wished you to know that, following the performance last night, I insisted on having her come and reside at my family's home. I have assigned two of our drivers to serve as her bodyguards until she is safe on the ferry back to France. Both of them are retired Royal Marines, are armed at all times, and will never let any harm come to anyone under their care.

She asked me to send her apologies for not being entirely forthcoming in her conversation with you. In truth, she is not only the niece of Mr. Serge Diaghilev. She is also a distant member of the Czar's family and for reasons of state cannot allow her true identity to become known. Her passion for ballet is overwhelming, and her mother agreed to allow her to join Les Ballets Russes only if Diaghilev agreed to keep her safe from all harm.

Please, sir, do not consider it required of you to follow her again today or during the rest of the week. She will be safe.

Again, my thanks, and please know that I am honored beyond all I could ask or imagine to have been able to assist in a case of Mr. Sherlock Holmes and Dr. Watson.

Yours very truly,

Thomas Stapleton-Cotton (Tom)

I leaned back in my chair and enjoyed a slow sip of my morning coffee. I could return to my medical practice with a clear conscience, knowing that Mr. Diaghilev's niece was in better hands than I could ever hope to provide. I might even find an hour or two to do some writing.

At five o'clock, I returned to Baker Street to find Holmes, yet again, poring over a cluster of texts and papers whilst gazing blankly at the score by Claude Debussy.

"Have you learned anything, Holmes?" I asked.

He sighed. "more than I ever imagined there was to know about this most unusual form of artistic expression."

"Indeed? Do tell."

"The ballet was invented centuries ago in Italy. It was adopted by the French, who provided it with an entire dictionary of terms, confirming my prejudice that the French do not care a whit what one does with one's body as long as one pronounces it properly. But nearly a century ago, the art form was adopted by the Russians, and they have continued to nurture it and train the world's finest ballet dancers up until the present day. And they did so not just in the Court in St. Petersburg or the mansions of Moscow. Every Russian village and town lays claim to its own ballet school, local company, and performance hall. The same is true for their orchestras. It has been quite the revelation to such as I who must humbly admit to thinking that all those Slavs, only recently released from universal serfdom, were only a small rung above cave dwellers."

"That makes," I said, "for interesting history, but what about those strange numbers. Where do they fit in?"

"*That*, I do not yet know. We know that the numbers in the first line give us a date and time. If the letters 'C' and 'G' refer to Covent Garden, as you suggested and I take as a distinct possibility, then the following numbers may give directions from Covent Garden to a meeting place somewhere else in the West End. But ... the numbers in the first column range from one to twelve. Those in the second from one through twenty-four. And third from one through ten. Obviously, they cannot be linked to basic ballet positions. There are only five of those. Several of the more difficult moves, such as the *arabesque* have numbered variations, but again they do not rise above five. The human body only has four limbs, and thus there are a limited number of contortions that even the most advanced dancer can assume. The stage has eight designated locations, beginning with the center of the stage at the front and moving in a clockwise direction to stage front-left, halfway back the stage on the left and so on. But there are only eight. So, it cannot be them."

"What about to a repetition of the movements?" I suggested. "We watched Mathilde Kschessinska do thirty-two fouettés, did we not. Wasn't she magnificent?"

"Indeed, she was. But she did them all in the same place. Now, some of the moves, those that involve running leaps, a *grand jeté*, for example, may take a dancer some distance, but only two or at the most three are performed in succession before he or she runs out of room on the stage. The standard stage for ballet is only forty feet wide and thirty-two feet deep. No, there must be some other code to these numbers."

He said no more and returned to his books and the score.

"I regret," he said, "having agreed that we would dine with the Countess at Simpson's. I would have preferred to spend more time trying to deduce the meaning of the code. Nevertheless, it is possible that, given the unpredictable directions of her brain and conversation, she might spark an insight in my mind. We can always hope."

Holmes's hope was futile. Countess Betsy was radiant and charming and predictably banal. The dinner, however, was excellent. We departed the restaurant and walked over to Bow Street with sufficient time to spare for Holmes to ensconce himself in seats provided for us by Mr. Diaghilev in the Dress Circle. He spread the score of *Après Midi* on his lap and took out a set of opera glasses. Several sharpened pencils could now be seen protruding from the breast pocket of his suit.

As soon as the curtain lifted, he began to scribble furiously on to the score. As a decent musician himself, he was fully capable of reading music and following along in the score with what he was hearing from the orchestra. In the limited light, I could make out that he was recording the body positions of the dancers as they changed with the progression of the music. His concentration was intense, and at one point, I saw him using two pencils at once, one in each hand. Fortunately, the ballets as choreographed by Nijinsky did not entail many rapid changes in body position. Most of the movements were intended to be slow and sensual, emphasizing the subtext of sexual attraction. Holmes appeared to be capturing every movement of all of the eight figures on the stage.

The response of the audience on the second night of this unusual ballet was more enthusiastic than the opening night. I assumed that those who had read the reviews and concluded that the performance would be offensive had decided against coming, leaving those who considered themselves to be amongst the self-appointed clique of the progressive and enlightened.

My second viewing of *Swan Lake* was every bit as thrilling as the first. This time around, I knew what was going to happen and was able to watch the dancers more closely as they positioned themselves for the moves they were about to make. Whereas the previous evening, my attention was captured by the extraordinary display of the lead dancers, this time I marveled at the precision uniformity of the *corps de ballet*. Sixty swans all moved as if they were a single being. Watching them was truly an awe-inspiring experience.

As on opening night, there was a short intermission after the end of *Après Midi* and a longer one part-way through *Swan Lake*. At the beginning of the second break, Holmes leaned toward my ear.

"Enjoy the rest of the evening, my friend. I must get to work on what I have recorded."

With that, he quickly made his way up the stairs to the upper lobby and vanished.

In spite of my vain protests of the late hour, the Countess prevailed upon me to join her for an after-theater repast at the Savoy. I had resigned myself to listening to her flamboyant nonsense but, to my surprise, she was all business. Not so much that it diminished her appetite, but in between mouthfuls of baked egg cocotte, rare breed sirloin, and lemon tart, she held forth on what she had been doing over the past few days.

"Doctor, my darling, Perhaps, you think I am nothing more than an amusing diversion for your brilliant friend—"

"Not at all, Countess," I interrupted. "You are a woman of the world with a rare set of exceptional gifts."

She laughed. "I hope you are more honest with your patients than *that*. Otherwise, they would all be dead by now. No Doctor, what I am is a farm girl from Wisconsin who is not afraid of hard work and willing to give diligent service to my employer, regardless of who he or she may be. Doing so has gotten me where I am now while my cousins are still milking cows and making cheese."

Now I laughed. "Somehow, Countess, I just cannot see you in that role."

"Neither can I. But now I must be serious. Our mutual friend, Mr. Sherlock Holmes, hired me not just to be his translator but also his informant. And so, I have spent all day, every day, trying to pry information out of the dancers and the other members of the company that might give me something to bring back to Mr. Holmes. I pretended to be the travel agent responsible for booking their passage back to Paris. That way, I can ask them very personal questions about the food, they will and will not eat, and who they will and will not share a cabin with, and which of the hunters is sleeping with which of the swans, and so many other things. Once a young girl tells me about her intestinal digestive problems because of foods that do not agree with her, it is easy to get her to tell me about everything else as if I were her mother fussing over her. I have worked faithfully at this task since I met with you and Mr. Holmes earlier this week."

"Excellent. And what have you learned."

"Everything and nothing."

"You will have to be more explicit."

"Well … since you asked … every time I pay a visit to the rooming house where the young women are living, I spot one or more of those people who were at the reception. They are also watching the place or attempting to be nonchalant while they chat with the girls."

"Yes, as in?"

"There are at least a half-a-dozen Russian men whose suits do not fit them properly. They are either diplomats or spies—which are, of course, one in the same—or members of the Czar's secret police. Then there are those anarchist boys, who quite frankly seem far more interested in flirting with the swans than in recruiting for the revolution. And to my surprise, Mrs. Cubitt has dropped in twice along with a translator, a priest borrowed from the Dormition Church."

"Goodness, what would she want with the ballerinas?" I said.

"You tell me, doctor. But even stranger has been Romola Nijinsky. You know, that former Miss de Pulszky who married Nijinsky in Argentina. She's been chatting up both the young men and the young women for the past two days."

I sat back, bewildered. "This is becoming utterly indecipherable. I am tempted to suggest to Holmes that he should declare a plague on all their houses and send them packing. It all makes no sense whatsoever. But then there is the matter of the two murdered dancers. What to make of them?"

"You tell me. You're the doctor."

I could not. We enjoyed the rest of the late dinner, and I bade her good night. When I returned to Baker Street, Holmes was nowhere to be found. So, I went to bed.

Chapter Nine

Running Out on The Nutcracker

Thursday evening marked our third night in a row at the ballet. This time, however, as it was now less than a month until Christmas, at least in England, if not in Russia, *Les Ballets Russes* put on a performance of *The Nutcracker*. It was again preceded by the short ballet, *Après midi d'un faun*, and I suspected that the scores of young mothers who were standing around in the lobby were waiting for that performance to end before bringing their little darlings to watch the joyful celebrations of Clara and Fritz.

I had not seen Holmes all day, and he was not even present at supper. I met Countess Betsy in the lobby, and together we waded our way through the throngs of children and to our seats in the Dress Circle. To my surprise, Holmes was already sitting in his seat with Debussy's score yet again open on his lap.

"Good evening," I said pleasantly, but before I could add anything to my greeting, Holmes raised his hand, palm facing me, and made it clear that he did not wish to be disturbed.

"Sorry, my friends," he said, speaking to the score, not to us. "Kindly do not disturb me. I may be on to something."

Throughout the short performance, he scribbled furiously, constantly drawing small lines with arrowheads at one end in the space above the staves. It made no sense at all to me, so I watched the strange ballet for what I hoped would be my last time.

At the first intermission, the Countess and I rose to make our way to the bar. Holmes remained seated, looking intently at the score that was now covered with arrows, stickmen in various contorted poses, and written notes. I offered to bring him a glass of Champagne.

"No. I need my mind to be completely clear." Then, as if, remembering his manners, he hastened to add, "But I thank you all the same. Please enjoy yourselves."

After the intermission, the families swarmed into the hall. Little girls in pretty dresses could be seen, and heard, everywhere. The decibel level rose accordingly. Holmes was

oblivious to the cacophony, and, at the beginning of the *Ouverture miniature,* he unfolded what appeared to be a map of London and spread it out on one knee whilst still balancing Debussy's score on the other.

He continued to ignore what was taking place on the stage. The children dancers did their delightful entrance, and he did not bother even to look up. The same for the entrance of Drosselmeyer, then toy soldiers, and then the waltzes of the parents and the grandparents.

Just as the stage darkened and the audience was hushed, watching Clara rise from her bed and return to the Christmas tree to retrieve her cherished Nutcracker, Holmes suddenly spoke a loud "Yes!" and pounded his thigh with his palm. Several heads turned to look at him. Several minutes later, as the hungry mice were terrorizing poor Clara, he let out another "Yes!" but even louder and highly inappropriate, considering what was taking place on the stage.

Fortunately, we were in the front row of the balcony, so could not disturb anyone sitting directly in front of us, but several mothers sitting behind us muttered their "shuuuush" in his direction.

The tableau faded and opened again with Nijinsky appearing as the nutcracker who was transformed into the handsome prince and our local princess, Miss Hilda Munnings, born and bred in the suburbs of London, appearing as the grown-up Clara. The audience burst into applause, and the dancers began their lovely *pas de deux*. Just seconds before the number ended, with the orchestra fading and the prince lifting Clara high above his head, Holmes let out a very loud,

"AH HA!!"

It could be heard throughout the theater. Now even those who were sitting in the orchestra section below us turned around to look up.

Holmes was on his feet.

"Watson. Come. Now," he commanded.

"Holmes," I pleaded, in a stage whisper. "Sit down. There are only the snowflakes to come before intermission."

"No! We have to go now." He had grabbed my arm and was forcefully tugging on it.

"Countess," he said to the horrified Betsy. "Tomorrow at Baker Street at nine. Be there. Oh ... and enjoy the rest of the evening. Watson! We have to go now."

If looks could have killed, we would have been slain several times over by half the mothers and matrons in the audience. Once we climbed up the steps in the dark, pushed our way past the ushers and through the doors, and entered the upper lobby, I turned to Holmes.

"Holmes! Are you mad? What has gotten into you?"

"I have solved it! Come. We need to get out of here and up to Covent Garden."

He was already moving toward the staircase, and I followed him down to the street level and out on to Bow Street. It was a clear, cold, early winter night, and I struggled to pull on my coat, gloves, and scarf on as we walked quickly—Holmes was nearly running—down Bow to Russell Street and then turned right into Covent Garden.

"St. Paul's is around the other end, facing the main entrance," Holmes shouted back at me. "That is where we start."

That much made sense. The first line of the cryptic numbers told us that. So, we pushed our way through the flower girls and food carts that were waiting for the exodus from the surrounding theaters, and, a few minutes later, we were standing at the main door of Covent Garden, looking across the piazza at the pediment front of a church.

Holmes was on fire. He was still carrying his coat over his arm whilst looking at the score in one hand and his map in the other. It was cold enough that I could see the vapor from his quick breaths as he stood. I caught up to him, forcibly removed his coat from his arm, and held it out behind him, ordering him to pull it on.

"Right. Thank you, Watson. Now look, this is where we go from here."

"Holmes," I said. "For pity sake, slow down and explain yourself."

"It finally became clear. Look at the score. See the numbers? Those are rehearsal numbers, references that the conductor, musicians, and dancers use to find their way around the score quickly. They're printed at the top of the page and again above the first violin staff. There are twelve of them."

He held the score open in front of me and quickly flipped through the twenty or so pages.

"Each section contains anywhere from four to seventeen bars of music. You may need your eyeglasses, but you can see that I have put a small number at the top of each bar."

I quickly pulled out my glasses and looked closely. Holmes had written a tiny number above each bar. His numbering started over with each section. Some sections were longer, others quite short.

"Last night, I tracked the ballet positions that the dancers assumed with each bar of music," he said. "But it made no sense. Their positions were utterly non-traditional, and many were altered whilst standing in the same position on the stage. The only dancer who was moving about the stage was the faun. This evening, I marked his movements from one location on the stage to another. At various times he moves from upstage to downstage, or stage left to stage right. And occasionally diagonally across either a portion of the stage or the entire expanse. I have recorded each direction and distance on the score."

"Yes," I said, not at all sure what this meant.

"Let us begin. Here we are at the front door of Covent Garden, where the code tells us we start."

"Yes."

"That first set of numbers reads 6 – 4 – x 2. We turn to section six, the fourth bar. At that point in the music, the Faun moves forward from center stage and dances downstage to stage location One, the front and middle, just before the apron. Had he come much further, he would be in the orchestra pit. He moves a distance of thirty-two feet."

"How do you know that?"

"Elementary, my dear Watson. Remember, the standard stage is thirty-two feet deep by forty feet wide. Thus, the distance from the center to the front is sixteen feet, and doing that distance twice is thirty-two feet. Now, if we walk forward that same distance from the front door of Covent Garden, it brings us out to the pavement of the west piazza, just in front of the church. Our second instruction reads: 7 – 13 – x 3. If we look at the score, I have noted that beginning at the thirteenth bar of the seventh section, he began in location seven of the stage, at the front and far stage right. He then turned to his right—and bear in mind that stage right and stage left are according to how they are seen by the audience, not by the actors or dancers—and traveled all the way from there across the entire front of the stage, a distance of forty feet which, when multiplied by three becomes one hundred and twenty feet. If we now turn to our right, we traverse the piazza and end up at the edge of King Street. It makes perfect sense."

"Holmes," I protested. "It may make sense, but it took you days to decipher. How are those dancers going to follow the code? They will not have all your scribbles and arrows in front of them."

"They will not need it. The map of the short ballet is written in their memories. Do I need a copy of a musical score to play Barcarolle one more time on the violin? Did any of the dancers during the past three evenings need a page of instructions telling them what steps to take, what positions to hold? Of course not. Do you need a medical text to tell you how to deliver a baby? Those dancers have danced *Après Midi* dozens of times. They know exactly who moves from place to place, and when in the music they do so, and they can all read music. Their bodies retain the memory of the dimensions of the stage. For them, it is like reading a nursery rhyme. For anyone else, it is meaningless. Really quite ingenious. Now follow me."

The next set of numbers took us right along King Street to the corner of James. There we turned left and followed the code up James to Long Acre. From there, it was right to the odd-shaped intersection of Long Acre with Bow and Endell Streets.

"Here," said Holmes, "we do as the Faun did and move on an angle, just as he did when dancing from stage location six back to center-stage-front, location eight."

"How do we know how far to go?" I asked.

"One of two ways can be used. We may, if we choose, make us of Pythagoras's theorem as moving from location six to position eight involves a hypotenuse. The one side is half the depth of the stage, therefore sixteen feet. The other side is twenty feet, being half the width of the stage. The sum of the squares is six hundred and fifty-six. The square root of that is twenty-five and six tenths plus an inch, perhaps."

"You are putting a tax on my brain, Holmes. It has been a very long time since I struggled through my maths back in school."

"Well, then we could do it the easy way, if you insist."

"And what is that?"

"Just look at the short section of road in front of us. It stops not far ahead and then turns. We go to where it stops and then follow the next direction."

"Right. That is somewhat easier."

Doing so took us through the intersection, and then we turned left on to Long Acre and subsequently followed it all the way out to Drury Lane. The next instruction had a high multiple, and we turned left on Drury Lane and followed it all the way to High Holborn. Another right and another high multiple led us to the intersection of New Oxford Street. We followed that to the east as far as Southampton Row, where we were instructed to turn back south two short blocks to Gate Street. Moving as the Faun had during the eleventh section of the musical composition, we walked a short block and a half along the narrow Gate Street.

We were now out of instructions but had found ourselves standing at the door of an old ale house whose sign proclaimed *The Ship Tavern. Founded in 1549.*

"Capital. Just capital," exulted Holmes. "Had we known the movements, we could have found our way here in under fifteen minutes. I think we can be quite certain that this is the location of the meeting tomorrow when the fate of Mr. Diaghilev's company shall be determined. Come, let us investigate the place."

He walked in as he spoke. The place was very old and lined with dark oak panels and heavy tables. There were a few windows at the front of the main room, but the remainder was well lit with relatively new electric light fixtures. At the back of the room was a set of doors that opened into a smaller room in which chairs were set up to accommodate up to forty people."

"Most likely," said Holmes, "a favorite place for meetings of union locals or branches of fraternal organizations. Mark my words; tomorrow at eleven o'clock, it will be filled with Russian dancers. If we disguise ourselves, we should be able to sit at this table right beside the door and overhear everything that is said."

"They will be speaking Russian," I said.

"That is why the Countess will be with us."

"In disguise? Her?"

"It will take some application of imagination, but I am certain I can provide something appropriate."

"She will die before she lets you dress her as a buxom madam."

Holmes nodded and sighed. "Some bribery may be required."

Chapter Ten

Eavesdropping on the Secret Meeting

At twenty minutes past nine the following morning, the bell sounded on Baker Street, followed by the yipping and yapping of a small dog and a set of slow, deliberate footsteps.

"Sheerlock, daahlink. You know, I really should not even be speaking to you," said Countess Betsy as she strode into the room and let down her tiny beast, assuming it would not run off in search of the nearest RSPCA officer.

"It is utterly unacceptable to run off and leave a lady sitting alone in a theater. And *you*, Dr. Watson. You did so too. I might have expected it from Sherlock, but never from you."

I smiled in return. "My dear Countess, matters of great importance to the Empire were at stake, and had we been so indiscreet as to inform you of same, the Foreign Office might have deported you back to Wisconsin. And we would not have wanted that, now would we?"

She laughed back at me. "No, Doctor, anything but that. Even English cuisine—an oxymoron if ever there was one—is better than cheese three times a day. Very well, I forgive you both. Now, what is it we have to do today that required me to rise at such an ungodly hour in the morning?"

"You will be joining us, and we shall be spies," said Holmes.

"Impossible," she replied. "Nothing in London worth spying on happens before three o'clock in the afternoon."

"We shall be spying on Russians."

"Then make that four o'clock."

"Young Russians."

"They do not even go to bed, at least to sleep, before six o'clock in the morning. They are too busy with ... well ... you know."

"The young Russian dancers from *Les Ballets Russes.*"

"But Sherlock, dahlink, they all know me. I have been engaging in intimate chats with them for the past two days."

"That is why all three of us must be in disguise. Please wait a minute."

Holmes got up and retreated to his bedroom. A minute later, he reappeared with a red velvet gown over his arm, and he laid it out over the back of the sofa. Even to my eye, I could see that the front of it was daringly low cut.

"Sherlock! I will not! Not even east of Aldgate would I be caught dead wearing something like that."

Holmes laid a wig of flaming red hair down beside the gown and then withdrew his wallet and added two ten-pound notes beside it.

"No one will recognize any of us. However, your utmost extended concentration shall be required. I trust we are in agreement."

"Is an elegant lunch included?"

"We shall be in a pub just off Holborn."

"Horrors ... Very well. I shall do it, but only because I adore you, dahlink."

We arrived at the Ship Tavern at ten-thirty and took the table Holmes had selected adjacent to the meeting room in the back of the pub. Holmes had dressed himself and me to match the Countess. The three of us could have passed for two sketchy pimps dividing the income from the previous evening with the local madam. The front section of the room was occupied by retired chaps who were still devouring their full English. A few of them looked up at us, ignored us, and returned to their sausage and baked beans.

"As we have a few minutes before they arrive," said Holmes, "would you mind, Watson, entering the meeting room and speaking a few words from the front as if you were addressing a full room of listeners?"

I did and recited a few familiar lines, beginning with "Friends, Romans, countrymen ..." and then returned to our table.

"Excellent," said Holmes. "You could be heard loud and clear. Now, if the two of you wish anything to eat, kindly order it now. Our young friends should be here by eleven o'clock."

The young friends did not arrive.

Eleven o'clock came and went, and not a single young Russian dancer had appeared.

Holmes was visibly agitated. At twelve minutes past eleven, he rose and walked back out the door to the pavement and stood and stared in the direction of the Kingsway for a full minute. He returned to our table, shaking his head.

"I appear to have failed in my deduction. But it seemed the only possible interpretation."

He sat down and lit a cigarette in an effort to calm his spirit. At twenty minutes past the hour, he extinguished it and pushed his chair back from the table as if to stand up and depart. Then his facial expression changed. He was looking in the direction of the door and smiling. I turned and looked as well and noticed two young men, both tall, slender, and Slavic-looking, who had just appeared.

"Ah ha," said Holmes quietly. "Eleven o'clock was not the hour at which they were supposed to arrive here, but the hour at which they departed Covent Garden. Likely, all the departure times were staggered so that they would not walk together and arrive en masse. Quite astute on behalf of the organizer."

Over the next half-hour, twos and threes of the members of *Les Ballets Russes* came through the pub and made their way into the meeting room and began to chatter amongst themselves.

"What are they talking about?" Holmes demanded of the Countess.

"They are young," she said. "What do you think they would be talking about? The boys are bragging about how much they had to drink after the performance last night. The girls are talking about their costumes and their sore feet and wondering what has happened to Tanya and Lukasha. They are all complaining about the food here in England and telling stories about where you can find a decent meal of zakusky and bliny. They are teasing each other and flirting. They are not old and serious like you, dahlink. Just be patient."

By eleven-fifty, nearly sixty people had gathered in the room. All the seats were taken, and several of the young men were standing along the wall at the back. Holmes was seated so that he could see who was still entering the pub. Countess Betsy and I had our backs to the door. At eleven fifty-five, Holmes's eyes went wide, and his lips parted. The other two of us adjusted our chairs and bodies nonchalantly so we could see what had grabbed his attention.

Three adults were entering the room. I recognized them from the reception Sunday night. They were the Russian Ambassador, the head of the Okhrana, and Mrs. Elsie Cubitt. They walked purposely through the pub and entered the back room. All chatter ceased, and the entire room stood up as they made their way to the front and sat in chairs that had been left vacant. One of the older male dancers came over to them, bowed, leaned over, and chatted briefly. Then he turned and stood to face the silent room. He addressed them in Russian. Betsy leaned in to the middle of the table and began her whispered translation.

"Brothers and sisters of Ballets Russes: Congratulations, I can see that you were all able to understand the code, follow my instructions, and come to this meeting. Now, my friends, it is my honor to introduce our Ambassador, His Excellency, Graf Sergey Semionovich Uvarov."

His words were followed by polite applause. Then there was a pause before the next speaker began. I could not see the speaker, but his voice was older and confident.

"Children of Mother Russia, I address you in the name of Nicholas the Second, the Emperor of All Russia ..."

"And then," said the Countess, "he says all the required things about the Czar and the glorious country. You know. Ah, now he starts ..."

"You have all been brilliant emissaries for your country. You have introduced first the French and now the English to the

great culture of Russia and, in particular, to our magnificent tradition of classical ballet, for which Russia is by far the most developed in the entire world. You have done this well. All of France and England and now even in the Americas they speak with great respect and admiration of the culture of Russia. The Emperor, all of his family, and all of Russia are very proud of you."

She paused. "He is just flattering them. That is what diplomats do before they ask you to do something ... ah, now he is getting to the point."

"We know that you have experienced great trials and tribulations over the past few months. We understand that Sergei Pavlovich Diaghilev is, at times, a difficult man to work for. This is common with many men of genius. We are, like you, very disappointed that he will not allow Vatslav Fomeech Nijinsky to continue to be a member of Les Ballet Russes. And we also understand why some of you, with nothing but loyalty to Mother Russia in your hearts, have come to us and said that the Emperor should recall Sergei Pavlovich Diaghilev to Moscow and let Les Ballet Russes continue with Vatslav Fomeech Nijinsky as the director..."

Again, the Countess paused. "Are they crazy? Nijinsky as director? He is now saying many nice things about Nijinsky. Now he stops and has to speak truth again"

Whilst she was listening, her eyes widened, and she muttered, "Oh no, that is sad."

"We all agree that he is the best dancer in the entire world, but just because he is the best dancer it does not mean that he is

a good choice to be director. And there is something else we must, with great sadness, tell you. We have had Nijinsky examined by doctors. Good doctors. French doctors, English doctors, and even we brought a Russian doctor. They are all agreed that Vatslav Fomeech Nijinsky is not well in his mind. His behavior and the things he says are not just because he is a passionate artist, it is also because his sanity is failing him. The doctors agree that madness is slowly overtaking him. It is possible that he will recover, but it is not likely. We all pray for a miracle, but we cannot act responsibly, hoping that one will take place."

The fellow stopped speaking for a moment, and we could hear murmuring, and then the quiet sobs of some of the young women. Then came the awkward muffled sounds of young men trying to hold back their tears.

"For these reasons, we want you to know that we have heard and sympathized with your concerns and your suggestions. For the time being, however, we have decided, and Emperor and Empress themselves support this decision, that we must allow Sergei Pavlovich Diaghilev to continue to lead Les Ballets Russes. We will have words with him and remind him that he must not show disrespect to his dancers and that he must pay your wages on time and that he must keep his private life private. However, it is best at this time that his decision not to have Vatslav Fomeech Nijinsky continue as a member must be respected. It is better for all of you, and it is better for Mother Russia if we do this. We have also met with the very great lady, Mrs. Cubitt, and we thank her for coming to this meeting. And we thank Anyushka for translating for her. She has assured us that one of her theaters, either the Royal Opera or the Royal

Drury Lane, will be available again for use by Les Ballets Russes next year at this same time."

He stopped, and again we could hear a growing volume of murmurs and whispering.

"Da. Yes. You wish to say something, young man. Speak. And speak freely. You may say what is in your heart. Your loyalty to the Emperor is not in question. Speak."

"It is," said the Countess, "one of the male dancers who now speaks."

"Excellency, we thank you for meeting with us and for your understanding and sympathy. We are all saddened to hear the news about our friend and brother Vaslav. There is, however, another matter of great concern to us, and we need to make you aware of it."

"Da, speak. We are listening."

"We have received messages, bad messages, threats, from someone we do not know, but they are all saying the same thing. They are demanding that we abandon not only Sergei Diaghilev but the company itself. They have said to us that after the performance this evening, there will be no more Ballets Russes. It will be gone, destroyed. These messages have nothing to do with the health of Vaslav or the behavior of Sergei. We cannot say for certain, but we think they sound like they come from someone who is criminal. We are all dancers, and we will perform because that is not only our duty but our passion. But, Excellency, please understand, we are also afraid. Already two of us have gone missing. Sergei has said that Tatiana and Luka have run away back to Paris because they are lovers, but we do

not believe this. We see the fear in his eyes when he says this to us. We know Tanya and Lukasha. They are our friends. We know they are lovers, but they are also dancers, and they would never run away from their duties to Les Ballets Russes. We fear for them. We fear for ourselves. Please understand us on this matter and do not say think that we are being cowards. Many of us have fathers who served the Emperor's army and who proudly wear the medals for their courage. But we know that something evil is taking place here in London. We need to know that we have not only your sympathy but your protection."

The young fellow stopped speaking. Various versions of "*Da*" could be heard from the gathered crowd. The Ambassador called for their attention.

"We have heard rumors of these threats, and we are very troubled as well. My Deputy, Nikolai Nikitich Demidov, assures me that he will have men at the theater this evening. He will have men to guard you at your residences. You will be protected until you depart on the ferry back to France on Sunday. You will be safe. We make this promise to you. Now, please, continue to be brave and be great dancers. Tonight, you perform a very difficult ballet. It is brilliant. Vatslav Fomeech Nijinsky and Igor Fyodorovich Stravinsky have created a masterpiece. It is very modern, and Russia needs for you to show England that we are not only the greatest in the music and ballet of the past but also will lead the world into dance and music that is new. And after you give a great performance, we can all relax and listen to the English musicians, and their orchestra do their best to play The 1812. It will be a great evening."

"He is now calling," said the Countess, "for a meeting with the leaders of the company to come and talk to him and the Deputy. He is telling the rest of them to go and enjoy a terrible English lunch of fish and chips, and mushy peas served on yesterday's newspaper."

There was a burst of laughter and a round of appreciative applause. Then the room broke up into general conversation. I took a quick peek inside the room and could seek that the crowd had stood up and had formed into clusters of friends, all chatting. A small group was at the front, standing around the Ambassador and his deputy. Another small group, almost entirely young women, had formed around Mrs. Elsie Cubitt and, with admiration written all over their lovely young faces, were happily bantering back and forth with her.

Within a few minutes, the dancers began to leave the room, generally looking cheerful. I was prepared to do the same. His Excellency's mention of a hot pub lunch, even if in jest, had aroused my appetite. Holmes, however, was not moving. He had brought his hands up in front of his chin and assumed a very familiar pose. His fingertips were pressed together, and he was scowling.

"This is not what I was expecting," he said. "I had hoped that we would be able to listen in on a meeting between the villains and those dancers who were thinking of throwing their lot in with them and defecting. Instead, we have a group of earnest young patriots who appear to care as much about their country as they do for each other and an Ambassador who, on the surface at least, cares about his young citizens."

"Sherlock, dahlink, do you think the Ambassador is being truthful?"

Holmes paused before answering that one. "One does not reach the elevated position as Ambassador of the Imperial Court of St. Petersburg to the Court of St. James's by spending the past twenty years telling the truth. He may have ulterior motives and certainly is privy to some facts of which we know nothing. He did appear genuinely concerned about the threats to the dancers. Of course, it would reflect badly on him if something untoward were to happen to them, the pride and joy of Russia, and it took place on his watch."

"Will he be able to protect them?" I asked.

"Possibly. Possibly not," said Holmes. "So, come now. We need to find Lestrade and make sure he has trained officers guarding them as well."

Chapter Eleven

Break a Leg,
May the Sets Fall Down

At seven o'clock that evening, Holmes and I met with Chief Inspector Lestrade at the Sir John Falstaff pub in Covent Garden.

"I would hope," said Lestrade, "that your predictions about tonight are right, Holmes. I have twenty men, half in uniform and half not, who will be scattered throughout the theater waiting for something to happen because Sherlock Holmes says it might. You better be right."

Holmes smiled back at his old compatriot. "My dear Lestrade. You really should be hoping that I am completely wrong and that the evening passes without anyone, citizen or foreign, receiving a scratch."

"Cut it out, Holmes. You know what I mean."

"I do, and I sincerely wish I had more specific suspicions to give you, but I do not. Only that it makes sense that whoever it is—and we do not know who they are—will do something—and we do not know what—this evening. If nothing happens, they will have lost their chance to destroy *Les Ballets Russes,* and we are operating only on very questionable evidence of their intentions. The alternative, however, to stand by and let them do something horrific, is not permissible. Is it, Inspector?"

"And where," asked Lestrade, "are you going to be all evening?"

"Unless required elsewhere, I shall be in my seat in the Dress Circle enjoying the performances."

Lestrade grunted. "From what I've heard that new ballet they are doing is like having alley cats screeching in the orchestra pit and the inmates of Bedlam going wild on the stage."

"I fear something close to that is how the critics will report it. However, Beecham's rendition of *The 1812* should be stirring. If nothing else, your men will enjoy that. Please remind them not to arrest the chaps sent by the Russian Embassy. They are supposed to all be on the same side."

At fifteen minutes before curtain time, we met Countess Betsy outside the Royal Opera House and entered the house yet again, our fourth consecutive night at the theater.

"Sherlock, my dear, you had better not abandon me again this evening," said the Countess, "or I may never speak to you again. And if you say something smart like 'Is that a threat or a promise?' I might just impale you with my hatpin."

Holmes looked at her warmly. "I shall consider myself a most fortunate gentleman indeed if I am honored to sit beside you throughout the entire performance."

"That's good, dahlink. Of course, I might get up and walk out if the new ballet is as horrendous as rumor has it."

"Ah, but will you return for Tchaikovsky?" replied Holmes.

"Only if you promise to finally take me back to the Savoy for my dinner afterward."

"I promise. Sometime after the performance, it is for certain that you shall be my guest."

We took our seats, and Holmes quietly opened the small valise he had been carrying and handed me a cloth bag, pulled tight at the top by a drawstring.

"Please use these," he said.

I opened the small sack to find a substantial set of field glasses, such as might be used by the Royal Navy.

"They are not," said Holmes, "as elegant as small opera glasses, but these binoculars are much more powerful. Once the house lights are lowered, no one will notice you anyway. Kindly keep scanning the audience, the stage, and the orchestra and alert me if anything seems unusual."

The audience was much livelier than normal, and I could hear snippets of animated conversation, all talking at once about the *avant-guard* and quite risqué ballet we were about to watch and the reputation of the music which "*that Russian, Stravinsky*" had composed. Soon, the house lights were dimmed, and the audience fell silent. A round of applause was given as Thomas Beecham entered, gave a practiced bow, and assumed his place in front of the orchestra. Then there was silence.

In the dim light, I could see the orchestra conductor make a small movement with his outstretched hand. Then a quiet, almost imperceptible sound could be heard. Some single instrument that I could not identify was playing an eerie melody. It was joined by first one and then several other instruments, but they were not playing in harmony. They were in discord, yet there was something about the discord that made it compelling. The music became louder and louder, and then the curtains opened.

On stage were several clusters of men, some standing together, others sitting or crouched together on the ground. The accented strings began to throb, but not in any consistent rhythm. I could hear three beats, followed by two beats, followed by nine and then five. The timpani pounded. The group of standing men started to jump up and down in time with the beats. A female dancer, dressed as an old crone, started making wild and awkward movements. She roused the rest of the huddled men, who joined the others and jumped and flailed their arms in unison. From the back stage-right wing, a string of females entered, also dressed as primitive peasants but not performing any dance step I had ever seen before. They were also jumping and stomping and flailing.

And it did not stop. The drums kept beating. The music was all in discord. And the dancers kept jumping and stomping, and falling down, and embracing the ground, and getting up and stomping some more.

"Holmes," I whispered. "What is *this*?"

He was gazing at the stage, positively enthralled. He whispered back without looking at me.

"My friend, you are witnessing the arrival of the future. They are *making it new*."

I took up my binoculars and kept scanning the house and the stage. I could not resist the temptation of looking at some members of the audience. Some were horrified. Others radiant.

The intermission mercifully arrived. Kissing the earth and becoming one with it and the strutting of a bearded old man had ended. I could not imagine what they would be doing in the second half. I was about to get up and make my way to the bar for a much-needed drink when I felt Holmes's hand on my forearm.

"Sorry, my friend. But I need you to continue to watch this crowd, especially now. If anyone is going to do something, it will most likely begin to unfold whilst the audience is up and moving around. Please keep looking for anything unusual."

The drink would have to wait. I picked up my binoculars and began watching all the antics that people carry on whilst they think no one is watching. Husbands were arguing with their wives, who, in turn, were either laughing with or arguing with other wives. One lady was fixing her hair whilst an overly large gentleman was conducting excavation operations on his left nostril. It was getting rather tedious, and the heavy navy binoculars had become a burden to my arms and wrists. I was about to set them aside when my gaze was frozen.

"Holmes. Front left corner of the orchestra section. Going through the door. See him?"

I handed him the binoculars, and he looked in that direction but doing so was futile. The man I had tried to point out to him had exited through the door that leads to the off-right wings.

Holmes put down the binoculars and looked at me, wanting an explanation.

"I cannot say for certain," I said. "I may be imagining things, but that chap, even though he was wearing decent clothes, looked for all the world like the thug who grabbed Miss Veronika."

"Did you see where he came from?"

"No. I just caught him in my sight as he crossed the hall in front of the orchestra pit. He was walking purposefully but not in a hurry. He just worked his way through the crowd who were standing in that corner and exited through the door. Nobody took notice of him."

Holmes stood up. "Come with me. Bring your binoculars."

He then turned to Countess Betsy. "My dear, in all probability, we shall return shortly. Certainly, in time to enjoy *The 1812.*"

She gave a loud, haughty harrumph and did not bother looking up at him.

We made way back up the stairs from the Dress Circle, across the upper lobby and down the theater's far stairwell. I followed Holmes as he took me all the way to the basement, through a labyrinth of hallways and back up another narrow set of stairs. When I recovered my bearings, I found myself standing in the far corner of the off-right wing. A few dancers were standing around along with a dozen or more stagehands. Back against the wall, two large Slavic-looking fellows were leaning back against the brickwork, their arms folded across their chests. There were also four of London's police force in uniform, standing more or less at attention.

"Is Lestrade here?" I whispered to Holmes.

"Somewhere," he whispered back.

I followed him until we were standing beside one of the policemen. Holmes leaned his head near to the fellow's ear.

"Constable. My name is Sherlock Holmes. Is Inspector Lestrade back here with you?"

The policeman beamed a cheerful smile at Holmes. "An honor to meet you, Mr. Holmes. And you must be Dr. Watson. An honor, gentlemen. Yes, the Chief Inspector was here a few minutes back, but he went through the crossover to the other wing. You can probably find him there, but I warn you, he's in a foul mood. Didn't like the music he had to listen to. Not one little bit, he didn't."

"Thank you. Excellent advice. We shall leave him in his crankiness. Now then, constable, did you happen to see a chap come back here who was not one of the Russian bodyguards and did not seem to fit in with the company?"

"They are all a bit odd back here, Mr. Holmes. What might he have looked like?"

Holmes looked over at me.

"He was about your height and size," I said. "He was wearing a black suit and a dark shirt. Black hair and had the look of a nasty chap from Whitechapel."

The policeman gave me a blank look. "Sir, you are describing almost every one of these blokes back here. Only difference is that the stagehands are a bit undernourished, and the bodyguards all look like they served as foot soldiers under Ivan the Terrible. Can't say as I noticed any one of them acting strange. They are all running back and forth and not making a sound. Up and down the ladders, they go pulling the ropes and dropping the sets and getting ready to hop out on the stage and change things around. But that's what all these fellows do, sir."

As we were standing there, a voice far above us shouted. "Heads! Large, heavyset flying down to center stage."

A chorus of "*Thank you* and *spasibo*" was returned by the dancers and the stagehands. I looked up into the fly tower and watched as an enormous thing was lowered slowly to a spot somewhat upstage of the center. Several chaps gathered around it as it descended and guided it into place.

"What in heaven's name is that?" I asked one of the stagehands.

"It's the altar," he said. "That's where they sacrifice the Chosen Virgin. They put her right up on top of it and leave her there. After the curtain, we bring her a ladder so she can climb down."

The set, now that I could see it, was painted to look like a pile of rock and boulders. The top of it, sitting about seven feet above the floor, was flat. That made sense to me. You cannot very well have sacrificial virgins rolling off.

"All these fellows," said Holmes, "seem legitimate. Come, we shall investigate the other wing. Stay out of their way on the stage. We can use the crossover behind the cyclorama."

Holmes appeared to be thoroughly familiar with the activity and arrangement of the backstage world. I reminded myself of an observation I had made many years ago, that the stage lost a fine actor when Holmes became a specialist in crime. I followed him behind the enormous painted canvas that hung just in front of the back wall of the stage, and we moved over to the other wing. Lestrade was standing there, looking unhappy.

"If this," said Lestrade, "is what music and dance are becoming, I have no hope for the next generation. Making my lads watch and listen to this nonsense is beyond belief."

"*The 1812*," said Holmes, "is coming. Only one more act to endure. Have you or your men observed any unusual activity back here."

"If you had asked me, Holmes, if I had observed anything *usual*, it would be easy to answer. The answer would be 'no.' But no one has been waving a gun or a knife or tossing dynamite, if that is what you are asking me."

The dancers were moving into a definite line-up, obviously about ready for the second act to start. As they did so, a young man took his place behind one of the leg curtains. He was dressed in a fine suit and climbed up onto the top of a small podium, rather like one of the preachers who stand on their soapbox at Hyde Park Corner. A closer look at him indicated that it was Vaslav Nijinsky.

"What's he doing there?" I asked Lestrade.

"He stays there right through the whole act. He gives directions to all the dancers, and when the music is too hard to follow, he shouts out the beat so they can keep in time. Seems to know what everybody is supposed to be doing out there."

"He should," said Holmes. "He created it."

The general dull roar from the house suddenly went silent, and I assumed that the house lights had dimmed. A minute later, I heard a polite round of applause and concluded that Beecham had again entered and given his bow to the audience. In the darkness of the wing, a group of the young women dancers silently moved from the wing and onto the stage.

The music began.

Again, a strange instrument played an eerie solo. It was joined by a few strings and woodwinds, again in discord.

The main curtain parted. The stage was dark. Then the lights brightened ever so slightly to reveal a circle of young women in peasant dress standing in front of the stone altar. In unison, they started to move around the circle, all swaying their arms, heads, and legs in coordinated movements, but unlike any ballet moves I had ever seen. Every so often, they stopped, went up *en pointe* all together and back down again, and returned to their strange circling routine.

They kept this up for several minutes. Now and again, I could see one of them and then another cast a quick look at Nijinsky, who was gesticulating constantly with his hands and arms, indicating the type of movements the dancers were supposed to be doing. He then stopped making circles in the air and started to weave his hands back and forth. The dancers complied and started to weave in and out and exchange their positions in the circle. They then kept this up for another several minutes.

Then the stage lights brightened. The weaving stopped, and there was just one beautiful, slender young woman standing in the middle of the circle. The rest of them were dancing, if you can call it that, in place and directing their movements in her direction.

The audience gave a round of applause.

"What was that for?" I whispered to Holmes.

"It's for the local girl, Hilda Munnings. She is the Chosen Virgin," he whispered back.

"What happens to her?"

"She is sacrificed on the altar."

Merciful heavens, I thought to myself. But then I remembered that in almost every ballet and opera, some young woman has to die before the finale.

The drums began to beat. In time with them, the dancers began to jump, and stomp, flail their arms, slap their thighs, and drop to the floor, and pop up again. The music became louder and louder.

Then the men reappeared, some were dressed as peasants, but several had added bearskins, with the animal's head sitting on top of their own. Slowly, in time with the incessant beating of the drums and thrumming of the other instruments, they moved, menacingly, around the Chosen Virgin.

She did not move. She stood, frozen in place as if transfixed with fear knowing that she would soon be ritually sacrificed so that the earth would give forth an abundant harvest and sustain the tribe through another year.

All of the dancers, men and women, were dancing around her, stomping and threatening. Again, this continued for several minutes and again became louder, insistent, disconcerting. And then the Chosen Virgin began to move. She did so with non-stop jumps and twists, bends, and stomps. At times she turned and turned like a whirling dervish but flailing and contorting at the same time. And she kept going and going and going.

"How can she keep it up," I whispered to Holmes. "She's going to dance herself to death."

"Precisely," he whispered back. "Please keep observing those who are backstage and not just the dancers."

Meanwhile, he was transfixed by the performance.

I raised the binoculars once more to my eyes and scanned the fly loft and rigging and the high catwalks that allowed the fly men to walk back and forth far above the action of the stage. Nothing up there, I concluded. So, I shifted my gaze to the fly gallery on the far side of the stage and, in the limited light, perused the distant catwalk adjacent to the locking rail whereon all the manila ropes had been tied, securing the dozen or more batons and dangling sets that were stored in the fly tower.

I was not at all sure of what I was seeing, and in a familiar if non-sensical move, I lowered my binoculars and looked in the same direction with my naked eye.

"Holmes," said, loud enough to be heard above the clamorous music. "Look."

I pointed to the catwalk high above the other wing and handed him the binoculars.

There was a man up there, and he was acting very oddly. Twice, I saw a tiny flash of light, as if reflected off of a small polished object.

"What is he doing?" I said.

"I cannot tell," Holmes replied.

"Should we do something?"

"Not yet. It may be nothing, and it would not do to interrupt the finale."

On the stage, the Chosen Virgin was continuing to dance like a crazed person. Turning, jumping, turning, dropping, rising, leaping. It was exhausting to watch her. Then, in time with a crash in the music. She dropped her body to the stage and lay prone. Then, one last convulsion and finally motionless. Dead.

The male dancers circled her, bent down, and slid their hands under her limp body. Together, they slowly lifted her up and up until the men's arms were stretched out above their heads, and the woman was being borne high in the air toward the altar. All of the dancers moved in and did slow movements indicating worship and obeisance. The Chosen Virgin was laid, lifeless, on the high altar.

I felt Holmes's elbow in my ribs. He was pointing to one of the largest sets held by the rigging above the stage. Unlike all the other units up there, it was no longer hanging level. One end had dropped several feet, and it was swaying and jerking.

"Dear God," gasped Holmes. "He's cutting the lines."

The same massive set was now bouncing up and down like an off-balance teeter-totter; first one end dropping and bouncing back up and then the other.

"There's only one line left," shouted Holmes.

He ran the short distance until he was beside Nijinsky on his podium. The brilliant dancer was utterly absorbed with the action on the stage, and Holmes swatted him on the leg to get his attention. Nijinsky glared down at him and shouted something in Russian, which I was certain was a rather abusive oath. Again, Holmes hit him and pointed up into the fly loft. For several seconds, Nijinsky looked up, completely confused. Then a look of horror came over his face, and he began shouting at the dancers.

The music of the finale was too loud. They could not hear him. I looked again up to the far fly catwalk. Whoever it was up there was moving his arm back and forth. He was cutting the final line that was holding up a massive set.

Holmes rushed up beside me and drove his hand into my pocket, and pulled out my service revolver. He stepped out of the legs and onto the stage, pointed the gun at the altar set, and began firing. The sound of the retorts exploded through the theater and were more than loud enough to be heard by the dancers. They all looked over at what appeared to be a madman shooting at them. On mass, they turned and ran toward the other wing.

Screams came from the audience, and people were jumping out of their seats.

The Chosen Virgin was still lying on the altar.

Nijinsky saw her.

With inhuman speed, he leapt off of his podium and ran across the stage. I watched as he did a shallow crouch whilst running, and then, like a tremendous gazelle, he jumped. It was a *grand jeté*, his one leg stretched forward and well above the level of his head. His foot hit the top of a painted boulder some six feet above the stage. His forward momentum carried him on up to the top of the altar.

He stooped over and put his arms around the waist of the Chosen Virgin and yanked her up off the altar. Her face was a picture of shock and disbelief.

The audience was now screaming.

Nijinsky leapt off the altar to the stage floor, landing and somersaulting forward, the Chosen Virgin in his arms.

A split second after he landed, an enormous set, the forest scene from the *Nutcracker* of the previous evening, came smashing down onto the altar, crushing it. Pieces of wood and paper maché and wire mesh exploded across the stage. Some of it landed in the orchestra pit. Some hit Nijinsky and the young woman as they were staggering to their feet.

Pandemonium had broken out in the house. Women were screaming. Men were shouting. Bodies were already running toward the exit doors.

Nijinsky had lifted the ballerina to her feet, and as I watched, he shouted something in her ear. She looked completely bewildered. He shouted again.

Then Hilda Munnings of Wanstead, England, the Chosen Virgin, walked as only a ballerina can toward the apron of the stage, dropped to one knee, and bowed gracefully. Nijinsky walked up beside her and bowed. Then he shouted to the far wing of the stage. Several seconds later, the entire troupe of dancers stomped and jumped their way to the front of the stage and bowed.

The screaming in the house suddenly vanished. After a few moments of stunned silence, the audience broke into a thunderous roar. Cheers, whistles, and endless loud shouts of 'bravo' filled the theater. I shook my head in disbelief.

Meanwhile, Holmes and Lestrade had gathered several of the police officers, and together they ran across the stage to the other wing, trying to reach the bottom of the fly loft ladder

before the man who had cut the lines could descend and escape. He must have seen them coming. I could see several of them pointing up into the fly tower and shouting. A dark figure was running across the fly tower catwalk back to the wing where I was standing.

A larger group of officers now rushed back across the stage, accompanied by several of the Russian bodyguards.

It must have looked extremely strange to the audience, who were still cheering and clapping for the dancers. The decibel level increased to deafening when the second charge came back across the stage.

The desperate villain had descended the ladders and now jumped the remaining ten feet to the floor by the far wall of the wing. The Russian bodyguards who had not crossed with the first charge swarmed upon him and would have beat him half to death had not the London Police officers arrived, pushed the Russians aside, surrounded the would-be assassin, and put a set of handcuffs on him.

I recognized him. For certain, it was the same thug who had tried to kidnap Miss Veronika. I shouted my observation above the continuing roar from the house to Lestrade. He did not appear to hear me.

Lestrade made motions with his hands commanding us to follow him out the back exit, along with his perpetrator and several of London's finest. As we worked our way to the back-corner door, we came face to face with Serge Diaghilev.

"*Godpodin* Holmes! What have you done to me!? First, you give me heart attack, and then you make me and *Ballets Russes* most famous act in all London. Good thing I go back to Paris. The French are crazy but not as crazy as what happen tonight. I am never forget this night as long as I live."

"May I assume," said Holmes, "that your satisfaction with my work will mean that you will pay my fee promptly and in full?"

Diaghilev arched his head back with a look of exaggerated shock. "Oh, *Godpodin* Holmes, if only you had accepted me as client instead of tell me is not possible because you work for Scotland Yard. I would pay you ten time what they pay, but you will not allow. I am so sad. But I send you bottle of best Russian vodka as token of my thank you. Whenever you drink it, you think of me."

He laughed heartily, gave Holmes a friendly, hard smack on his back, and disappeared down the stairs to the basement and the dressing rooms where his dancers were now recovering from their shock. We caught up with Lestrade out on the pavement behind the theater.

Chapter Twelve

The Race to Southampton

"That was a near run thing, Holmes," said Lestrade. "Lucky for us that dancing fairy fellow could jump like that."

"He is," said Holmes, "rather famous for that skill."

"Right. Well, I will have this madman taken down to the station and charged. Have to say, I am happy you helped track him down. Glad to have this round of nonsense over with."

"Inspector ... I fear it is far from over. Do you truly believe that this monster did all that of his own accord?"

Lestrade glared at Holmes and then shrugged and sighed.

"Go enjoy the rest of the performance. And meet me at the Yard first thing tomorrow morning."

Holmes and I quickly made our way back up to our seats just a moment before the doors were closed. The entire theater was still abuzz with chatter. It would be a long time before they stopped talking about the explosive final scene of *The Rite of Spring*.

Thomas Beecham re-entered and gave his bow. The talking subsided. We took our seats beside the Countess.

"Sherlock, where have you been, darling?" she whispered somewhat more loudly than necessary. "What you missed! I am so sorry darling, that you were not here to watch it. *Oh bozhe*, you would not believe how those crazy Russians ended their wretched ballet."

"Sssshh," said Holmes. "You can tell us all about it after the overture has ended."

The orchestra's rendition of the famous piece of music was stirring, and they even included several house-shaking live canon blasts at the twelve-minute mark and ear-splitting church bells as it ended. On any other night, their use might have been the talk of the town the next day. Tonight, they were met with polite applause. As soon as the clapping had ended and the audience began to stand and prepare to depart, the talk returned to the shared thrill of the end of the ballet.

Over an exquisite after-theater dinner at the Savoy, Countess Betsy delivered an animated and perhaps exaggerated account of the end of the ballet which, so tragically, Holmes and I were not in our seats to enjoy. Holmes smiled at her coyly throughout.

In the taxicab on our way back to Baker Street, I could tell that his mind was elsewhere. Before parting to our rooms for the night, he turned to me.

"Thank you, my dear friend, for all your assistance with this case. However ..."

"However," I interrupted him. "It is not over. And yes, Holmes, I shall be ready first thing tomorrow morning to accompany you to Scotland Yard."

"Ah, good old Watson. Have I ever told you ..."

"Yes. Many times. Good night, Holmes."

***

Seven-thirty the following morning found us in Lestrade's office on the Embankment.

"His name he says is Jack Ferguson," said the Chief Inspector. "From Sussex, but now lives in London, past Brick Lane. Spent a few years in Broadmoor for being crazy as well as bad. Now he works as a thug for hire. We thought he would be an easy one to crack, but he's a clever devil."

"And why do you say that?" asked Holmes.

"Straight away his makes up a story that he was hired by the Russians to cut the ropes and that the entire thing was staged. No one was hurt, so where is the crime? It's his word against that dandy Russian impresario. Who do you think a jury would believe?"

"Ah, yes. There might be a problem on that front," said Holmes. "Would you mind terribly, Inspector, if I had a word with him?"

"Go ahead. My boys put his arse in a wringer for three hours, so I do not think you can do much more."

We followed Lestrade down to the cells in the basement. A guard opened the door to the cell in which a young man, dressed in a dark shirt and dark suit, was relaxed on a cot, with his back leaning against the wall. He was smoking a cigarette, and his free hand was resting on his stomach. He had a bandage on his thumb.

"Good morning, Jack," said Holmes. "It has been a while. How have you been?"

At first, the fellow looked puzzled and then a flash of recognition followed by a cold glare of hatred.

"What are you doing here, Sherlock Holmes?' he demanded.

"I need your help, Jack."

"I spent five years in the nuthouse because of you. You won't get anything from me. I already told the coppers everything. I didn't do no crime, and now they have to let me out."

"Oh dear. That is unfortunate. You see, Jack, it is not just about last night. Do you recognize my colleague, Dr. Watson?"

"Good morning, Jack," I said. "We met down in Lamberley. Your father was an old school chum of mine."

"I know who you are," he snarled. "I remember you."

"Excellent," said Holmes. "However, it appears that Dr. Watson also remembers you as the man who kidnapped a young woman off the streets of London a few days ago and is prepared to identify you as such in a court of law. I understand that your eyes were being attacked at the same time, so you would not have had a good look at the man who rescued the young ballerina."

The thug was now staring at me, but the smirk had gone from his face.

"Kidnapping, as you know, Jack," continued Holmes, "is a serious offense and carries a hefty sentence. However, what you did was so far beyond reason that a doctor of the mind would very likely testify that you are still not well in your head and need to be sent back to Broadmoor. You might need another five years. Maybe seven to recover your wits."

The fellow's face changed from insolence to panic.

"You wouldn't."

"Oh, I would not. But a magistrate would. Mind you, if I were to testify that you were merely under contract to someone else, it would likely sway his opinion."

"Blast you, Holmes. What do you want?"

"The identity of whoever hired you."

"I don't know."

"Oh, dear. That is unfortunate. Of course, we might have to charge you with murder as well."

"Bloody hell. No one was murdered. No one even got hurt, except for me when that vixen laid her teeth into my thumb."

"The other two dancers were shot in the head."

Now a look of horror swept across his face. "Shot? No. I had nothing to do with that. He just told me to get them and bring them to him. That's all I did. He said to take their wallets so that it would look like a robbery, and I did that and delivered them to him. That was all I did. They were both alive and kicking all the time. I never had nothing to do with hurting them. I swear."

"Where did you bring them?"

"Basement of some place in the West End. Brought them at night. It was dark."

"Who was he?"

"Don't know. No one ever gives a name; you know that. He hired me, and I did the job, and he paid me. No names."

"What did he look like?"

"Don't know. It was dark. Total dark. I couldn't see his face."

"How tall?"

"Can't say. It was dark. Told you that. Seemed about my height, but he could have been on a step. I don't know."

"His voice then. Did he have an accent? Russian? French? Irish?"

"He didn't talk. Just gave me a note with the offer and shone a torch on it. I said 'yes' and then he gives a paper with instructions, lights it up, and it says I have to memorize them, and then he takes it back."

"How much did he offer you?"

"Forty-one pounds, eight shillings, six 'p'. Odd amount, but that was what was written down."

Holmes stopped his questions, stood up, and began walking toward the door of the cell.

"Come," he said to me and Lestrade. "We do not have much time."

"Where are we going," I asked as I was almost running behind him.

"Waterloo. If we catch the 8:30 to Southampton, we can get there before she sails."

"Who sails?"

"The *Mauretania*. The murderer is likely getting on it now."

Lestrade disappeared into his office came rushing out a minute later.

"I don't know what you're up to, Holmes, but I know that look on your face. One of our cars will take us to Waterloo," he shouted as he hustled his way out of the building.

We were soon in a powerful police motor car and racing our way across the Waterloo Bridge. Halfway across, the traffic ground to a halt, and we crawled all the way to

Southbank. Holmes checked his watch constantly, but to my surprise, Lestrade calmly read a newspaper and seemed oblivious to the increasing likelihood that the train we needed to catch would have departed before we arrived at the station.

At 8:35, we pulled up to the front of Waterloo and sprang out. Holmes ran inside and looked up at the great board where the train times were displayed.

"We are in luck. It has been delayed. Who knows why, but it is our good fortune."

"Good fortune, my arse," said Lestrade. "Your good fortune would be better called a phone call from Scotland Yard telling them to hold the train."

In the first-class cabin, Holmes thanked Lestrade for his foresight and then spent most of the journey pacing up and down the corridor, smoking one cigarette after another. He was not in the mood to explain anything, and Lestrade and I had to content ourselves with speculative chat and reading the newspapers.

At the half-hour mark, the train made a brief stop at Woking Station. Lestrade excused himself and rushed off the train, returning just before the conductor called for all aboard. Lestrade was smiling, somewhat smugly.

"Holmes," he said. "You will be out of time to get on that ship and look for your villain before it casts off."

"We may have to stay on board after it departs. However, it makes a stop at Cobh, and, if necessary, we can disembark there."

"That will not be necessary," said Lestrade. "Departure has been delayed."

Holmes smiled at his colleague of many years. "Am I to conclude, my dear Inspector, that the Cunard Steamship Line has been ordered to delay the departure of their prize ocean liner?"

"Quite legitimate," said Lestrade. "Scotland Yard is going to carry out an inspection of their lifeboat drill to make sure they are complying with the new regulations that came into force this spring because of the tragedy of April of last year. Not going to have that happen again."

The great Southampton Docks were only a few blocks from the Central Railway Station, and a police vehicle was waiting for us. With its bell clanging, it sped its way right out on to the dock and pulled up alongside the gangplank. Once we were out on the pier, the chill wind reminded us that it was late November, and even though the sun was shining, it was cold standing out in the open. The ship's captain, Mr. John Pritchard, was waiting for us at the top of the walkway with a cluster of his officers. They were not looking at all happy. His language, as might be expected of an angry sailor, was somewhat colorful, and I confess to a bowdlerized account below.

"Since when," he bellowed, "does Scotland Yard conduct an investigation of a ship of state?"

Lestrade took him aside, and I assume confided to him the true reason for our discomfiting him and his crew. The captain nodded, turned to his officers and ordered them to move throughout the ship instructing every one of the passengers to assemble beside their designated lifeboats. His men looked exceptionally puzzled, but being good sailors all, went and did as they were told.

"What did you say to him?" I asked Lestrade.

"I told him that Sherlock Holmes and Scotland Yard both suspected that a crazy murderer was on board and either we tried to find him now or he was going to be on board all the way to New York. The captain thought it was rather a good idea that we found him now."

An officer appeared with the manifest of the passengers, and Holmes perused it carefully, shaking his head from one page to another. After looking over the final page, he handed it back, saying nothing. I knew without asking that whoever it was we were looking for must be traveling under a false name.

Twenty minutes later, the captain and two of his officers returned.

"They are all assembled," said Captain Pritchard. "We can start at the top with our First-Class folks. Don't want them too inconvenienced."

"Are they sitting on benches?" demanded Holmes. "Do they have blankets?"

The captain, in language that I shall not record, confirmed that they did.

"And no doubt," added Holmes, "are being supplied with Champagne, food and hot chocolate. We will start with the families on the lower decks. Follow me."

He turned and began walking toward the closest set of stairs. The captain looked as if he were about to explode. I happened to catch Lestrade's eye and knew that both of us were biting our lips, trying not to laugh.

The lifeboat stations for the third and steerage passengers were a hive of laughter and chatter in every language of Babel. Mothers and fathers were holding their babies and toddlers in their arms to keep them from the cold whilst the older children had managed to all find each other and, needing only the universal language of play, were engaging in tag and hide and seek and endless shrill giggles. When called to attention, however, the entire crowd fell silent immediately and responded promptly and clearly when they heard their names called.

I heard names from every country of Europe. Back before the turn of the century, most of these folks would have come from France, Sweden, Norway, Denmark, Iceland, Germany, and Great Britain, especially Ireland. Now they were overwhelmingly Italians, Greeks, Bulgarian, Romanians, Macedonians, Serbians, and Russians. A least a quarter of them were Jews. I took a moment to gaze at them in profound admiration, knowing that they were setting out to the New World to find a life and a future for their children. I could not but be in awe of their spirit and courage.

Within half an hour, we had completed the masses on the lower decks, and now, at the captain's insistence, we moved to the upper deck. The atmosphere could not have been more different. These well-dressed and blanketed folks were chatting amiably. I recognized some of them either from my medical practice or the society pages of the press. They were going to America for a pleasant holiday, much of which they might spend in the warmer climes of the southern states after they had shopped in New York. They generally ignored the officer's request for silence, and he had to shout some names out several times before getting an affirmative answer. As we walked past them, I could not help but hear a few of them exclaim something to the effect of "Oh my God, that's Sherlock Holmes. What is he doing on board?" That question was followed by, "Oh, isn't this a treat. We must have a nasty criminal on board. That will be a welcome relief to the boredom of the next week." A few shouted questions to Holmes as he passed by. He ignored them.

There were about five hundred passengers in the First Class, and we got through them in another twenty minutes. The captain announced that complimentary food and hot drinks would be served in the ballroom and dismissed them from the stations. That left the second class, of which there were another five hundred people.

Many of these passengers were tradespeople, or those with some means and skills, and they were traveling to America either to start a new life and business or to engage in some type of commerce before returning to England. A surprising number were men and women of the Hasidic sector of the Hebrew faith. The men were immediately identified by the long dark coats, oversize Bowler hats, and the payots of hair dangling beside their ears. The older men had full grey beards. They were generally quiet and murmured to each other as they stood, huddled together against the wind.

An officer called out names, and answers came promptly. We moved quickly from station to station. All the while, Holmes said nothing and merely gave every one of them a quick once over with his eyes.

At the third station, we repeated the same drill, but as we were walking away, he turned around and strode quickly up behind one of the Hasidic fellows and, to my utter shock, gave the back of his head a hard swat, sending his hat flying. Shouts of horrified protest came immediately from the crowd, but Holmes then reached up and yanked at the fellow's hair. A close-cropped wig, complete with payots, came off in Holmes's hand. The man immediately began to run but was quickly tackled by two more of the Hebrew men.

"He is imposter," one of them shouted as they wrestled him to the ground. Four of them now man-handled him up to where Holmes and the rest of us were standing.

"Captain, Inspector," said Holmes, "allow me to introduce Mr. Gerald M. Coghlan, a rather wayward Irish Catholic, making his return to the Great White Way. May I suggest, Inspector, that if you have your men investigate his activities over the past few weeks, you will have grounds for charging him with murder."

A cluster of burly sailors picked up the disguised American and carried him off the boat, and handed him over to the police officers who were waiting on the pier.

Captain Pritchard turned to us and, refraining from any vulgar language, said, "We shall require a half an hour to get everything back in order before we cast off. May I welcome you as guests at my table until then?"

Chapter Thirteen

Elementary, My Dear Inspector

We had no sooner sat down and been handed snifters of a highly select brandy than Lestrade, as might be expected, demanded an explanation.

"We begin, as always," said Holmes, "with *cui bono*. There were several people who could have made a fortune by inducing the members of *Les Ballets Russes* to defect and join a new company in which the brilliant Nijinsky would continue to dance, but the talented yet impossible Serge Diaghilev would have no part. There is a considerable fortune to be made now that it has become so famous."

"Right," interrupted Lestrade. "We all know that. Now get on with it. How did you know it was him?"

"First, one must eliminate the other possible suspects," said Holmes, affecting an air of tedium. "Mrs. Cubitt has the funds and the ability to have a new version of *Les Ballets Russes* become the resident company in one of her theaters. She is an honorable woman who appears to have devoted her life to good deeds, but she is, after all, an American with a very checkered past. Nijinsky's sister, Miss Bronislava, is a brilliant dancer *and* choreographer, as well as a capable businesswoman and completely loyal to her brother. She might have tried to take control of the company and keep her brother as the lead dancer. Now you may be tempted to answer that both of these women are highly honorable, but I would remind you that the most winning woman I ever knew was hanged for poisoning three little children for their insurance."

"We've heard about her, Holmes," said Lestrade. "More than once."

"You occasionally need a reminder," said Holmes and then continued. "At first I thought the murders could have been ordered by the Russian Embassy if they suspected that the dancers were in league with the anarchists and dissidents. Or by the anarchists, if they suspected the dancers were in league with the Czar. God Almighty only knows what all intrigues that begin in St. Petersburg end up in London, and I suspect that at times even He gets confused. But we learned that the girl they tried to kidnap was a distant cousin of the Czar and royalty are

not in the habit of killing family members, at least not recently. And the starving dissidents were more concerned with their empty stomachs than the revolution.

"I fully expected that the secret meeting which we overheard would reveal the identity of the villains, only to have it turn into a sympathetic hearing by the Russian Ambassador and Mrs. Cubitt. That eliminated them. The money lenders had good reason to seize control of the company to protect their investments, and that fellow, Mr. Slainstein, remained on my list. But Mr. Coghlan moved to the top."

"Why?" demanded Lestrade.

"He had a very powerful motive in the form of a fortune in profit to be made if he were to poach the dancers, including the brilliant but dismissed Nijinsky, and take them all to America. You heard Diaghilev claim that ticket prices in New York could be quadrupled, and an enormous windfall could be made."

"Any one of them," said Lestrade, "could have made a fortune if they took control. I asked you, why the American?"

"Oh, I am sorry. I had thought that was obvious. The amount of the payment offered to Ferguson gave it away."

"Well now," said Lestrade, "I am sorry, but it is not at all obvious to me, so explain, Holmes."

"Why would anyone offer such an odd amount? The reason is that according to the rates of exchange for this week, as given in the early morning edition of the *Times,* forty-one pounds, eight shillings, six p is precisely one hundred American dollars. Only an American would offer that amount."

I glanced at Lestrade. He caught me looking at him, and we both rolled our eyes.

Holmes continued.

"Whilst in Diaghilev's hotel suite, I observed an exchange of looks between the two young boys and Coghlan, and it was obvious that some sort of connection existed between them. It is now reasonable to conclude that they were *his* spies and were the source of information to him concerning Diaghilev's spies."

"Right," said Lestrade, "Mind you, I had the impression that they were paid to be ... well ... affectionate to Diaghilev, if you know what I mean."

"A correct deduction, Inspector. And if you were them, would you not be more willing to work for someone who offered you *more* spending money *without* wanting anything else from you?"

"Well, I am not them," said Lestrade. "But I suppose you have a point there. Keep going."

"Had the disaster at the end of the *Rite of Spring*," said Holmes, "gone as planned, and several of the dancers either killed or grievously injured, *Les Ballets Russes* would have been in chaos. Bankruptcy would soon follow, and poaching the dancers and staff would have been easy pickings. With the failure of the plan, I suspected that the villain, most likely the American, feared that Jack Ferguson could give him away. Therefore, it was highly likely, although not certain, that he would attempt to escape from England on the first and fastest steamship available which, of course, was the *Mauritania*.

Thus, we raced to the docks to try to apprehend him before it departed."

"Fine. Just fine, Holmes," said Lestrade. "Not get to the part where you picked him out from two thousand passengers."

"Elementary, my dear inspector. His shoes."

Epilogue

The murderer, , Gerald M. Coghlan, was arrested and placed in jail He was, however, a man of means and had access to excellent lawyers. At the time of writing, he is out on bail, and his trial has been postponed yet again.

Les Ballets Russes returned to Paris without either Vaslav Nijinsky or his sister, Bronislava Nijinska. They both remained in London and attempted unsuccessfully to form another dance company. Nijinsky and his new wife then moved to Vienna, where, I am told, dismal events have overtaken their lives. When war broke out across Europe, Nijinsky, being classed as a Russian and, therefore, an enemy alien, was placed under house arrest. His mind, sadly, continued to deteriorate, and it will not be long before he will be confined to an institution for the mentally ill.

The English girl from Wanstead, Hilda Munnings, has changed her name to Lydia Sokolova, and continues to dance brilliantly, mainly in character roles, with *Les Ballets Russes*.

The handsome and courageous young lord, Tom, (now Sir Thomas Stapleton-Cotton) who helped rescue the abducted ballerina, has completed his studies and is running for a seat in Parliament. The lovely Miss Veronika has been replaced by a sensible if plain-looking English girl, foisted on Tom by his mother, who knew that dalliances with Russian dancers were fraught with danger.

Sherlock Holmes has expanded his appreciation of the arts and is now an enthusiastic follower of the ballet.

Dear Sherlockian Reader:

In 1909, Serge Diaghilev brought his company of classically trained Russian ballet dancers to Paris. From then until Diaghilev's death in 1929, they performed in Paris and toured throughout the world. Their impact on the universe of dance is unparalleled. They brought classical ballet back to the stage and introduced modern interpretive ballet to the universe of arts and letters. Many of the individual dancers, such as Ana Pavlova, Bronislava Nijinska, and George Balanchine, went on to found schools of ballet and subsequent companies.

Vaslav Nijinsky, now recognized as one of the most brilliant ballet dancers of all time, had a tragically short public career before his break with Serge Diaghilev and his subsequent descent into schizophrenia and a life spent in and out of mental institutions.

The information in this story about *Les Ballets Russes*, Serge Diaghilev, Igor Stravinsky, Vaslav Nijinsky, and the various other historical characters is generally accurate. Some names and dates have been altered to fit the narrative. The Russian dancers did introduce *Le Sacre du Printemps* to an audience in Paris in the spring of 1913, and a riot actually broke out in the Paris Opéra. They also performed it in London but did so before the fated tour to South America, not after.

References to murder, treachery, Scotland Yard and Sherlock Holmes are fictional.

However, while doing the research for the story, I learned that *Les Ballets Russes* had gone on a tour of South America during the summer of 1913. During that tour, Vaslav Nijinsky married Romola de Pulszky, bringing about the rupture of his relationship with Serge Diaghilev. They were married in the church of San Migual Arcangel, located on Suipacha Steet in central Buenos Aires. As I write these words, I am living on Suipacha Street, a few blocks north of the church and have been throughout the time of writing the story. Who knew? (I took the photo).

Serge Diaghilev was a brilliant and flamboyant impresario who was openly gay. He was what we would now call a "sugar daddy" to a long line of young male ballet dancers, including Nijinsky. He regularly stayed at the Savoy Hotel, and *Les Ballets Russes* performed in the Royal Opera House and the Royal Drury Lane Theatre while in London. (took this one too).

The Ship Tavern is still where it was in 1913, just off of High Holborn. You can walk to it from Covent Garden using the route provided in the story.

The *Mauretania*, one of the great ships of the Cunard Line, held the Blue Riband for many years. Lifeboat drills and adequate provision of life jackets and lifeboats were instituted following the *Titanic* disaster in the spring of 1912.

The ballets and music referred to in the story are still enjoyed by audiences throughout the world.

Simpson's Restaurant is still where it was on the Strand and is still a select dining establishment. (and this one).

Thank you for reading this New Sherlock Holmes Mystery. Hope you enjoyed it.

Warm regards,

Craig

Did you enjoy this story? Are there ways it could have been improved? Please help the author to improve the experience for readers of future stories by leaving a constructive review on the site where you obtained this book. Thank you. CSC

About the Author

In May of 2014 the Sherlock Holmes Society of Canada – better known as The Bootmakers – announced a contest for a new Sherlock Holmes story. Although he had no experience writing fiction, the author submitted a short Sherlock Holmes mystery and was blessed to be declared one of the winners. Thus inspired, he has continued to write new Sherlock Holmes Mysteries since and is on a mission to write a new story as a tribute to each of the sixty stories in the original Canon. He currently writes from Buenos Aires, Toronto, the Okanagan, and Manhattan. Several readers of New Sherlock Holmes Mysteries have kindly sent him suggestions for future stories. You are welcome to do likewise at: craigstephencopland@gmail.com.

New Sherlock Holmes Mysteries
by Craig Stephen Copland

www.SherlockHolmesMystery.com

"Best selling series of new Sherlock Holmes stories. All faithful to The Canon."

This is the first book in the series. Go to my website, start with this one and enjoy MORE SHERLOCK.

Studying Scarlet. Starlet O'Halloran, a fabulous mature woman, who reminds the reader of Scarlet O'Hara (but who, for copyright reasons cannot actually be her) has arrived in London looking for her long-lost husband, Brett (who resembles Rhett Butler, but who, for copyright reasons, cannot actually be him). She enlists the help of Sherlock Holmes. This is an unauthorized parody, inspired by Arthur Conan Doyle's *A Study in Scarlet* and Margaret Mitchell's *Gone with the Wind*.

Six new Sherlock Holmes stories are always free to enjoy. If you have not already read them, go to this site, sign up, download and enjoy.

Super Collections A, B and C

57 New Sherlock Holmes Mysteries.

The perfect ebooks for readers who subscribe to Kindle Unlimited

Enter 'Craig Stephen Copland Sherlock Holmes Super Collection' into your Amazon search bar. Enjoy over 2 million words of MORE SHERLOCK.

www.SherlockHolmesMystery.com

The Adventure of the Dancing Men

The original Sherlock Holmes Story

Arthur Conan Doyle

The Adventure of the Dancing Men

Holmeshad been seated for some hours in silence with his long, thin back curved over a chemical vessel in which he was brewing a particularly malodorous product. His head was sunk upon his breast, and he looked from my point of view like a strange, lank bird, with dull grey plumage and a black top-knot.

"So, Watson," said he, suddenly, "you do not propose to invest in South African securities?"

I gave a start of astonishment. Accustomed as I was to Holmes's curious faculties, this sudden intrusion into my most intimate thoughts was utterly inexplicable.

"How on earth do you know that?" I asked.

He wheeled round upon his stool, with a steaming test-tube in his hand and a gleam of amusement in his deep-set eyes.

"Now, Watson, confess yourself utterly taken aback," said he.

"I am."

"I ought to make you sign a paper to that effect."

"Why?"

"Because in five minutes you will say that it is all so absurdly simple."

"I am sure that I shall say nothing of the kind."

"You see, my dear Watson"—he propped his test-tube in the rack and began to lecture with the air of a professor addressing his class—"it is not really difficult to construct a series of inferences, each dependent upon its predecessor and each simple in itself. If, after doing so, one simply knocks out all the central inferences and presents one's audience with the starting-point and the conclusion, one may produce a startling, though possibly a meretricious, effect. Now, it was not really difficult, by an inspection of the groove between your left forefinger and thumb, to feel sure that you did NOT propose to invest your small capital in the goldfields."

"I see no connection."

"Very likely not; but I can quickly show you a close connection. Here are the missing links of the very simple chain: 1. You had chalk between your left finger and thumb when you returned from the club last night. 2. You put chalk there when you play billiards to steady the cue. 3. You never play billiards except with Thurston. 4. You told me four weeks ago that Thurston had an option on some South African property which would expire in a month, and which he desired you to share with him. 5. Your cheque-book is locked in my drawer, and you have not asked for the key. 6. You do not propose to invest your money in this manner."

"How absurdly simple!" I cried.

"Quite so!" said he, a little nettled. "Every problem becomes very childish when once it is explained to you. Here is an unexplained one. See what you can make of that, friend Watson." He tossed a sheet of paper upon the table and turned once more to his chemical analysis.

I looked with amazement at the absurd hieroglyphics upon the paper.

"Why, Holmes, it is a child's drawing," I cried.

"Oh, that's your idea!"

"What else should it be?"

"That is what Mr. Hilton Cubitt, of Riding Thorpe Manor, Norfolk, is very anxious to know. This little conundrum came by the first post, and he was to follow by the next train. There's a ring at the bell, Watson. I should not be very much surprised if this were he."

A heavy step was heard upon the stairs, and an instant later there entered a tall, ruddy, clean-shaven gentleman, whose clear eyes and florid cheeks told of a life led far from the fogs of Baker Street. He seemed to bring a whiff of his strong, fresh, bracing, east-coast air with him as he entered. Having shaken hands with each of us, he was about to sit down when his eye rested upon the paper with the curious markings, which I had just examined and left upon the table.

"Well, Mr. Holmes, what do you make of these?" he cried. "They told me that you were fond of queer mysteries, and I don't think you can find a queerer one than that. I sent the paper on ahead so that you might have time to study it before I came."

"It is certainly rather a curious production," said Holmes. "At first sight it would appear to be some childish prank. It consists of a number of absurd little figures dancing across the paper upon which they are drawn. Why should you attribute any importance to so grotesque an object?"

"I never should, Mr. Holmes. But my wife does. It is frightening her to death. She says nothing, but I can see terror in her eyes. That's why I want to sift the matter to the bottom."

Holmes held up the paper so that the sunlight shone full upon it. It was a page torn from a note-book. The markings were done in pencil, and ran in this way:—

Holmes examined it for some time, and then, folding it carefully up, he placed it in his pocket-book.

"This promises to be a most interesting and unusual case," said he. "You gave me a few particulars in your letter, Mr. Hilton Cubitt, but I should be very much obliged if you would kindly go over it all again for the benefit of my friend, Dr. Watson."

"Well, Mr. Holmes, what do you make of these?" he cried. "They told me that you were fond of queer mysteries, and I don't think you can find a queerer one than that. I sent the paper on ahead so that you might have time to study it before I came."

"It is certainly rather a curious production," said Holmes. "At first sight it would appear to be some childish prank. It consists of a number of absurd little figures dancing across the paper upon which they are drawn. Why should you attribute any importance to so grotesque an object?"

"I never should, Mr. Holmes. But my wife does. It is frightening her to death. She says nothing, but I can see terror in her eyes. That's why I want to sift the matter to the bottom."

Holmes held up the paper so that the sunlight shone full upon it. It was a page torn from a note-book. The markings were done in pencil, and ran in this way:—

Holmes examined it for some time, and then, folding it carefully up, he placed it in his pocket-book.

"This promises to be a most interesting and unusual case," said he. "You gave me a few particulars in your letter, Mr. Hilton Cubitt, but I should be very much obliged if you would kindly go over it all again for the benefit of my friend, Dr. Watson."

have not asked for the key. 6. You do not propose to invest your money in this manner."

"How absurdly simple!" I cried.

"Quite so!" said he, a little nettled. "Every problem becomes very childish when once it is explained to you. Here is an unexplained one. See what you can make of that, friend Watson." He tossed a sheet of paper upon the table and turned once more to his chemical analysis.

I looked with amazement at the absurd hieroglyphics upon the paper.

"Why, Holmes, it is a child's drawing," I cried.

"Oh, that's your idea!"

"What else should it be?"

"That is what Mr. Hilton Cubitt, of Riding Thorpe Manor, Norfolk, is very anxious to know. This little conundrum came by the first post, and he was to follow by the next train. There's a ring at the bell, Watson. I should not be very much surprised if this were he."

A heavy step was heard upon the stairs, and an instant later there entered a tall, ruddy, clean-shaven gentleman, whose clear eyes and florid cheeks told of a life led far from the fogs of Baker Street. He seemed to bring a whiff of his strong, fresh, bracing, east-coast air with him as he entered. Having shaken hands with each of us, he was about to sit down when his eye rested upon the paper with the curious markings, which I had just examined and left upon the table.

"I'm not much of a story-teller," said our visitor, nervously clasping and unclasping his great, strong hands. "You'll just ask me anything that I don't make clear. I'll begin at the time of my marriage last year; but I want to say first of all that, though I'm not a rich man, my people have been at Ridling Thorpe for a matter of five centuries, and there is no better known family in the County of Norfolk. Last year I came up to London for the Jubilee, and I stopped at a boarding-house in Russell Square, because Parker, the vicar of our parish, was staying in it. There was an American young lady there— Patrick was the name—Elsie Patrick. In some way we became friends, until before my month was up I was as much in love as a man could be. We were quietly married at a registry office, and we returned to Norfolk a wedded couple. You'll think it very mad, Mr. Holmes, that a man of a good old family should marry a wife in this fashion, knowing nothing of her past or of her people; but if you saw her and knew her it would help you to understand.

"She was very straight about it, was Elsie. I can't say that she did not give me every chance of getting out of it if I wished to do so. 'I have had some very disagreeable associations in my life,' said she; 'I wish to forget all about them. I would rather never allude to the past, for it is very painful to me. If you take me, Hilton, you will take a woman who has nothing that she need be personally ashamed of; but you will have to be content with my word for it, and to allow me to be silent as to all that passed up to the time when I became yours. If these conditions are too hard, then go back to Norfolk and leave me to the lonely life in which you found me.' It was only the day before our wedding that she said those very words to me. I told her that I was content to take her on her own terms, and I have been as good as my word.

"Well, we have been married now for a year, and very happy we have been. But about a month ago, at the end of June, I saw for the first time signs of trouble. One day my wife received a letter from America. I saw the American stamp. She turned deadly white, read the letter, and threw it into the fire. She made no allusion to it afterwards, and I made none, for a promise is a promise; but she has never known an easy hour from that moment. There is always a look of fear upon her face— a look as if she were waiting and expecting. She would do better to trust me. She would find that I was her best friend. But until she speaks I can say nothing. Mind you, she is a truthful woman, Mr. Holmes, and whatever trouble there may have been in her past life it has been no fault of hers. I am only a simple Norfolk squire, but there is not a man in England who ranks his family honour more highly than I do. She knows it well, and she knew it well before she married me. She would never bring any stain upon it—of that I am sure.

"Well, now I come to the queer part of my story. About a week ago—it was the Tuesday of last week—I found on one of the window-sills a number of absurd little dancing figures, like these upon the paper. They were scrawled with chalk. I thought that it was the stable-boy who had drawn them, but the lad swore he knew nothing about it. Anyhow, they had come there during the night. I had them washed out, and I only mentioned the matter to my wife afterwards. To my surprise she took it very seriously, and begged me if any more came to let her see them. None did come for a week, and then yesterday morning I found this paper lying on the sun-dial in the garden. I showed it to Elsie, and down she dropped in a dead faint. Since then she has looked like a woman in a dream, half dazed, and with terror always lurking in her eyes. It was then that I wrote and sent the paper to you, Mr. Holmes. It was not a thing that I could take to the police, for they would have laughed at me, but you will tell me what to do. I am not a rich man; but if there is any danger threatening my little woman I would spend my last copper to shield her."

He was a fine creature, this man of the old English soil, simple, straight, and gentle, with his great, earnest blue eyes and broad, comely face. His love for his wife and his trust in her shone in his features. Holmes had listened to his story with the utmost attention, and now he sat for some time in silent thought.

"Don't you think, Mr. Cubitt," said he, at last, "that your best plan would be to make a direct appeal to your wife, and to ask her to share her secret with you?"

Hilton Cubitt shook his massive head.

"A promise is a promise, Mr. Holmes. If Elsie wished to tell me she would. If not, it is not for me to force her confidence. But I am justified in taking my own line —and I will."

"Then I will help you with all my heart. In the first place, have you heard of any strangers being seen in your neighbourhood?"

"No."

"I presume that it is a very quiet place. Any fresh face would cause comment?"

"In the immediate neighbourhood, yes. But we have several small watering-places not very far away. And the farmers take in lodgers."

"These hieroglyphics have evidently a meaning. If it is a purely arbitrary one it may be impossible for us to solve it. If, on the other hand, it is systematic, I have no doubt that we shall get to the bottom of it. But this particular sample is so short that I can do nothing, and the facts which you have brought me are so indefinite that we have no basis for an investigation. I would suggest that you return to Norfolk, that you keep a keen look-out, and that you take an exact copy of any fresh dancing men which may appear. It is a thousand pities that we have not a reproduction of those which were done in chalk upon the window-sill. Make a discreet inquiry also as to any strangers in the neighbourhood. When you have collected some fresh evidence come to me again. That is the best advice which I can give you, Mr. Hilton Cubitt. If there are any pressing fresh developments I shall be always ready to run down and see you in your Norfolk home."

The interview left Sherlock Holmes very thoughtful, and several times in the next few days I saw him take his slip of paper from his note-book and look long and earnestly at the curious figures inscribed upon it. He made no allusion to the affair, however, until one afternoon a fortnight or so later. I was going out when he called me back.

"You had better stay here, Watson."

"Why?"

"Because I had a wire from Hilton Cubitt this morning—you remember Hilton Cubitt, of the dancing men? He was to reach Liverpool Street at one-twenty. He may be here at any moment. I gather from his wire that there have been some new incidents of importance."

We had not long to wait, for our Norfolk squire came straight from the station as fast as a hansom could bring him. He was looking worried and depressed, with tired eyes and a lined forehead.

"It's getting on my nerves, this business, Mr. Holmes," said he, as he sank, like a wearied man, into an arm-chair. "It's bad enough to feel that you are surrounded by unseen, folk, who have some kind of design upon you; but when, in addition to that, you know that it is just killing your wife by inches, then it becomes as much as flesh and blood can endure. She's wearing away under it—just wearing away before my eyes."

"Has she said anything yet?"

"No, Mr. Holmes, she has not. And yet there have been times when the poor girl has wanted to speak, and yet could not quite bring herself to take the plunge. I have tried to help her; but I dare say I did it clumsily, and scared her off from it. She has spoken about my old family, and our reputation in the county, and our pride in our unsullied honour, and I always felt it was leading to the point; but somehow it turned off before we got there."

"But you have found out something for yourself?"

"A good deal, Mr. Holmes. I have several fresh dancing men pictures for you to examine, and, what is more important, I have seen the fellow."

"What, the man who draws them?"

"Yes, I saw him at his work. But I will tell you everything in order. When I got back after my visit to you, the very first thing I saw next morning was a fresh crop of dancing men. They had been drawn in chalk upon the black wooden door of the tool-house, which stands beside the lawn in full view of the front windows. I took an exact copy, and here it is." He unfolded a paper and laid it upon the table. Here is a copy of the hieroglyphics:—

"Excellent!" said Holmes. "Excellent! Pray continue."

"When I had taken the copy I rubbed out the marks; but two mornings later a fresh inscription had appeared. I have a copy of it here":—

Holmes rubbed his hands and chuckled with delight.

"Our material is rapidly accumulating," said he.

"Three days later a message was left scrawled upon paper, and placed under a pebble upon the sun-dial. Here it is. The characters are, as you see, exactly the same as the last one. After that I determined to lie in wait; so I got out my revolver and I sat up in my study, which overlooks the lawn and garden. About two in the morning I was seated by the window, all being dark save for the moonlight outside, when I heard steps behind me, and there was my wife in her dressing-gown. She implored me to come to bed. I told her frankly that I wished to see who it was who played such absurd tricks upon us. She answered that it was some senseless practical joke, and that I should not take any notice of it.

"'If it really annoys you, Hilton, we might go and travel, you and I, and so avoid this nuisance.'

"'What, be driven out of our own house by a practical joker?' said I. 'Why, we should have the whole county laughing at us.'

"'Well, come to bed,' said she, 'and we can discuss it in the morning.'

"Suddenly, as she spoke, I saw her white face grow whiter yet in the moonlight, and her hand tightened upon my shoulder. Something was moving in the shadow of the tool-house. I saw a dark, creeping figure which crawled round the corner and squatted in front of the door. Seizing my pistol I was rushing out, when my wife threw her arms round me and held me with convulsive strength. I tried to throw her off, but she clung to me most desperately. At last I got clear, but by the time I had opened the door and reached the house the creature was gone. He had left a trace of his presence, however, for there on the door was the very same arrangement of dancing men which had already twice appeared, and which I have copied on that paper. There was no other sign of the fellow anywhere, though I ran all over the grounds. And yet the amazing thing is that he must have been there all the time, for when I examined the door again in the morning he had scrawled some more of his pictures under the line which I had already seen."

"Have you that fresh drawing?"

"Yes; it is very short, but I made a copy of it, and here it is."

Again he produced a paper. The new dance was in this form:—

"Tell me," said Holmes—and I could see by his eyes that he was much excited—"was this a mere addition to the first, or did it appear to be entirely separate?"

"It was on a different panel of the door."

"Excellent! This is far the most important of all for our purpose. It fills me with hopes. Now, Mr. Hilton Cubitt, please continue your most interesting statement."

"I have nothing more to say, Mr. Holmes, except that I was angry with my wife that night for having held me back when I might have caught the skulking rascal. She said that she feared that I might come to harm. For an instant it had crossed my mind that perhaps what she really feared was that HE might come to harm, for I could not doubt that she knew who this man was and what he meant by these strange signals. But there is a tone in my wife's voice, Mr. Holmes, and a look in her eyes which forbid doubt, and I am sure that it was indeed my own safety that was in her mind. There's the whole case, and now I want your advice as to what I ought to do. My own inclination is to put half-a-dozen of my farm lads in the shrubbery, and when this fellow comes again to give him such a hiding that he will leave us in peace for the future."

"I fear it is too deep a case for such simple remedies," said Holmes. "How long can you stay in London?"

"I must go back to-day. I would not leave my wife alone all night for anything. She is very nervous and begged me to come back."

"I dare say you are right. But if you could have stopped I might possibly have been able to return with you in a day or two. Meanwhile you will leave me these papers, and I think that it is very likely that I shall be able to pay you a visit shortly and to throw some light upon your case."

Sherlock Holmes preserved his calm professional manner until our visitor had left us, although it was easy for me, who knew him so well, to see that he was profoundly excited. The moment that Hilton Cubitt's broad back had disappeared through the door my comrade rushed to the table, laid out all the slips of paper containing dancing men in front of him, and threw himself into an intricate and elaborate calculation. For two hours I watched him as he covered sheet after sheet of paper with figures and letters, so completely absorbed in his task that he had evidently forgotten my presence. Sometimes he was making progress and whistled and sang at his work; sometimes he was puzzled, and would sit for long spells with a furrowed brow and a vacant eye. Finally he sprang from his chair with a cry of satisfaction, and walked up and down the room rubbing his hands together. Then he wrote a long telegram upon a cable form. "If my answer to this is as I hope, you will have a very pretty case to add to your collection, Watson," said he. "I expect that we shall be able to go down to Norfolk to-morrow, and to take our friend some very definite news as to the secret of his annoyance."

I confess that I was filled with curiosity, but I was aware that Holmes liked to make his disclosures at his own time and in his own way; so I waited until it should suit him to take me into his confidence.

But there was a delay in that answering telegram, and two days of impatience followed, during which Holmes pricked up his ears at every ring of the bell. On the evening of the second there came a letter from Hilton Cubitt. All was quiet with him, save that a long inscription had appeared that morning upon the pedestal of the sun-dial. He enclosed a copy of it, which is here reproduced:—

Holmes bent over this grotesque frieze for some minutes, and then suddenly sprang to his feet with an exclamation of surprise and dismay. His face was haggard with anxiety.

"We have let this affair go far enough," said he. "Is there a train to North Walsham to-night?"

I turned up the time-table. The last had just gone.

"Then we shall breakfast early and take the very first in the morning," said Holmes. "Our presence is most urgently needed. Ah! here is our expected cablegram. One moment, Mrs. Hudson; there may be an answer. No, that is quite as I expected. This message makes it even more essential that we should not lose an hour in letting Hilton Cubitt know how matters stand, for it is a singular and a dangerous web in which our simple Norfolk squire is entangled."

So, indeed, it proved, and as I come to the dark conclusion of a story which had seemed to me to be only childish and bizarre I experience once again the dismay and horror with which I was filled. Would that I had some brighter ending to communicate to my readers, but these are the chronicles of fact, and I must follow to their dark crisis the strange chain of events which for some days made Ridling Thorpe Manor a household word through the length and breadth of England.

We had hardly alighted at North Walsham, and mentioned the name of our destination, when the station-master hurried towards us. "I suppose that you are the detectives from London?" said he.

A look of annoyance passed over Holmes's face.

"What makes you think such a thing?"

"Because Inspector Martin from Norwich has just passed through. But maybe you are the surgeons. She's not dead—or wasn't by last accounts. You may be in time to save her yet—though it be for the gallows."

Holmes's brow was dark with anxiety.

"We are going to Ridling Thorpe Manor," said he, "but we have heard nothing of what has passed there."

"It's a terrible business," said the station-master. "They are shot, both Mr. Hilton Cubitt and his wife. She shot him and then herself—so the servants say. He's dead and her life is despaired of. Dear, dear, one of the oldest families in the County of Norfolk, and one of the most honoured."

Without a word Holmes hurried to a carriage, and during the long seven miles' drive he never opened his mouth. Seldom have I seen him so utterly despondent. He had been uneasy during all our journey from town, and I had observed that he had turned over the morning papers with anxious attention; but now this sudden realization of his worst fears left him in a blank melancholy. He leaned back in his seat, lost in gloomy speculation. Yet there was much around to interest us, for we were passing through as singular a country-side as any in England, where a few scattered cottages represented the population of to-day, while on every hand enormous square-towered churches bristled up from the flat, green landscape and told of the glory and prosperity of old East Anglia. At last the violet rim of the German Ocean appeared over the green edge of the Norfolk coast, and the driver pointed with his whip to two old brick and timber gables which projected from a grove of trees. "That's Ridling Thorpe Manor," said he.

As we drove up to the porticoed front door I observed in front of it, beside the tennis lawn, the black tool-house and the pedestalled sun-dial with which we had such strange associations. A dapper little man, with a quick, alert manner and a waxed moustache, had just descended from a high dog-cart. He introduced himself as Inspector Martin, of the Norfolk Constabulary, and he was considerably astonished when he heard the name of my companion.

"Why, Mr. Holmes, the crime was only committed at three this morning. How could you hear of it in London and get to the spot as soon as I?"

"I anticipated it. I came in the hope of preventing it."

"Then you must have important evidence of which we are ignorant, for they were said to be a most united couple."

"I have only the evidence of the dancing men," said Holmes. "I will explain the matter to you later. Meanwhile, since it is too late to prevent this tragedy, I am very anxious that I should use the knowledge which I possess in order to ensure that justice be done. Will you associate me in your investigation, or will you prefer that I should act independently?"

"I should be proud to feel that we were acting together, Mr. Holmes," said the inspector, earnestly.

"In that case I should be glad to hear the evidence and to examine the premises without an instant of unnecessary delay."

Inspector Martin had the good sense to allow my friend to do things in his own fashion, and contented himself with carefully noting the results. The local surgeon, an old, white-haired man, had just come down from Mrs. Hilton Cubitt's room, and he reported that her injuries were serious, but not necessarily fatal. The bullet had passed through the front of her brain, and it would probably be some time before she could regain consciousness. On the question of whether she had been shot or had shot herself he would not venture to express any decided opinion. Certainly the bullet had been discharged at very close quarters. There was only the one pistol found in the room, two barrels of which had been emptied. Mr. Hilton Cubitt had been shot through the heart. It was equally conceivable that he had shot her and then himself, or that she had been the criminal, for the revolver lay upon the floor midway between them.

"Has he been moved?" asked Holmes.

"We have moved nothing except the lady. We could not leave her lying wounded upon the floor."

"How long have you been here, doctor?"

"Since four o'clock."

"Anyone else?"

"Yes, the constable here."

"And you have touched nothing?"

"Nothing."

"You have acted with great discretion. Who sent for you?"

"The housemaid, Saunders."

"Was it she who gave the alarm?"

"She and Mrs. King, the cook."

"Where are they now?"

"In the kitchen, I believe."

"Then I think we had better hear their story at once."

The old hall, oak-panelled and high-windowed, had been turned into a court of investigation. Holmes sat in a great, old-fashioned chair, his inexorable eyes gleaming out of his haggard face. I could read in them a set purpose to devote his life to this quest until the client whom he had failed to save should at last be avenged. The trim Inspector Martin, the old, grey-headed country doctor, myself, and a stolid village policeman made up the rest of that strange company.

The two women told their story clearly enough. They had been aroused from their sleep by the sound of an explosion, which had been followed a minute later by a second one. They slept in adjoining rooms, and Mrs. King had rushed in to Saunders. Together they had descended the stairs. The door of the study was open and a candle was burning upon the table. Their master lay upon his face in the centre of the room. He was quite dead. Near the window his wife was crouching, her head leaning against the wall. She was horribly wounded, and the side of her face was red with blood. She breathed heavily, but was incapable of saying anything. The passage, as well as the room, was full of smoke and the smell of powder. The window was certainly shut and fastened upon the inside. Both women were positive upon the point. They had at once sent for the doctor and for the constable. Then, with the aid of the groom and the stable-boy, they had conveyed their injured mistress to her room. Both she and her husband had occupied the bed. She was clad in her dress —he in his dressing-gown, over his night clothes. Nothing had been moved in the study. So far as they knew there had never been any quarrel between husband and wife. They had always looked upon them as a very united couple.

These were the main points of the servants' evidence. In answer to Inspector Martin they were clear that every door was fastened upon the inside, and that no one could have escaped from the house. In answer to Holmes they both remembered that they were conscious of the smell of powder from the moment that they ran out of their rooms upon the top floor. "I commend that fact very carefully to your attention," said Holmes to his professional colleague. "And now I think that we are in a position to undertake a thorough examination of the room."

The study proved to be a small chamber, lined on three sides with books, and with a writing-table facing an ordinary window, which looked out upon the garden. Our first attention was given to the body of the unfortunate squire, whose huge

176

frame lay stretched across the room. His disordered dress showed that he had been hastily aroused from sleep. The bullet had been fired at him from the front, and had remained in his body after penetrating the heart. His death had certainly been instantaneous and painless. There was no powder-marking either upon his dressing-gown or on his hands. According to the country surgeon the lady had stains upon her face, but none upon her hand.

"The absence of the latter means nothing, though its presence may mean everything," said Holmes. "Unless the powder from a badly-fitting cartridge happens to spurt backwards, one may fire many shots without leaving a sign. I would suggest that Mr. Cubitt's body may now be removed. I suppose, doctor, you have not recovered the bullet which wounded the lady?"

"A serious operation will be necessary before that can be done. But there are still four cartridges in the revolver. Two have been fired and two wounds inflicted, so that each bullet can be accounted for."

"So it would seem," said Holmes. "Perhaps you can account also for the bullet which has so obviously struck the edge of the window?"

He had turned suddenly, and his long, thin finger was pointing to a hole which had been drilled right through the lower window-sash about an inch above the bottom.

"By George!" cried the inspector. "How ever did you see that?"

"Because I looked for it."

"Wonderful!" said the country doctor. "You are certainly right, sir. Then a third shot has been fired, and therefore a third person must have been present. But who could that have been and how could he have got away?"

"That is the problem which we are now about to solve," said Sherlock Holmes. "You remember, Inspector Martin, when the servants said that on leaving their room they were at once conscious of a smell of powder I remarked that the point was an extremely important one?"

"Yes, sir; but I confess I did not quite follow you."

"It suggested that at the time of the firing the window as well as the door of the room had been open. Otherwise the fumes of powder could not have been blown so rapidly through the house. A draught in the room was necessary for that. Both door and window were only open for a very short time, however."

"How do you prove that?"

"Because the candle has not guttered."

"Capital!" cried the inspector. "Capital!"

"Feeling sure that the window had been open at the time of the tragedy I conceived that there might have been a third person in the affair, who stood outside this opening and fired through it. Any shot directed at this person might hit the sash. I looked, and there, sure enough, was the bullet mark!"

"But how came the window to be shut and fastened?"

"The woman's first instinct would be to shut and fasten the window. But, halloa! what is this?"

It was a lady's hand-bag which stood upon the study table— a trim little hand-bag of crocodile-skin and silver. Holmes opened it and turned the contents out. There were twenty fifty-pound notes of the Bank of England, held together by an india-rubber band—nothing else.

"This must be preserved, for it will figure in the trial," said Holmes, as he handed the bag with its contents to the inspector. "It is now necessary that we should try to throw some light upon this third bullet, which has clearly, from the splintering of the wood, been fired from inside the room. I should like to see Mrs. King, the cook, again. You said, Mrs. King, that you were awakened by a LOUD explosion. When you said that, did you mean that it seemed to you to be louder than the second one?"

"Well, sir, it wakened me from my sleep, and so it is hard to judge. But it did seem very loud."

"You don't think that it might have been two shots fired almost at the same instant?"

"I am sure I couldn't say, sir."

"I believe that it was undoubtedly so. I rather think, Inspector Martin, that we have now exhausted all that this room can teach us. If you will kindly step round with me, we shall see what fresh evidence the garden has to offer."

A flower-bed extended up to the study window, and we all broke into an exclamation as we approached it. The flowers were trampled down, and the soft soil was imprinted all over with footmarks. Large, masculine feet they were, with peculiarly long, sharp toes. Holmes hunted about among the grass and leaves like a retriever after a wounded bird. Then, with a cry of satisfaction, he bent forward and picked up a little brazen cylinder.

"I thought so," said he; "the revolver had an ejector, and here is the third cartridge. I really think, Inspector Martin, that our case is almost complete."

The country inspector's face had shown his intense amazement at the rapid and masterful progress of Holmes's investigation. At first he had shown some disposition to assert his own position; but now he was overcome with admiration and ready to follow without question wherever Holmes led.

"Whom do you suspect?" he asked.

"I'll go into that later. There are several points in this problem which I have not been able to explain to you yet. Now that I have got so far I had best proceed on my own lines, and then clear the whole matter up once and for all."

"Just as you wish, Mr. Holmes, so long as we get our man."

"I have no desire to make mysteries, but it is impossible at the moment of action to enter into long and complex explanations. I have the threads of this affair all in my hand. Even if this lady should never recover consciousness we can still reconstruct the events of last night and ensure that justice be done. First of all I wish to know whether there is any inn in this neighbourhood known as 'Elrige's'?"

The servants were cross-questioned, but none of them had heard of such a place. The stable-boy threw a light upon the matter by remembering that a farmer of that name lived some miles off in the direction of East Ruston.

"Is it a lonely farm?"

"Very lonely, sir."

"Perhaps they have not heard yet of all that happened here during the night?"

"Maybe not, sir."

Holmes thought for a little and then a curious smile played over his face.

"Saddle a horse, my lad," said he. "I shall wish you to take a note to Elrige's Farm."

He took from his pocket the various slips of the dancing men. With these in front of him he worked for some time at the study-table. Finally he handed a note to the boy, with directions to put it into the hands of the person to whom it was addressed, and especially to answer no questions of any sort which might be put to him. I saw the outside of the note, addressed in straggling, irregular characters, very unlike Holmes's usual precise hand. It was consigned to Mr. Abe Slaney, Elrige's Farm, East Ruston, Norfolk.

"I think, inspector," Holmes remarked, "that you would do well to telegraph for an escort, as, if my calculations prove to be correct, you may have a particularly dangerous prisoner to convey to the county gaol. The boy who takes this note could no doubt forward your telegram. If there is an afternoon train to town, Watson, I think we should do well to take it, as I have a chemical analysis of some interest to finish, and this investigation draws rapidly to a close."

When the youth had been dispatched with the note, Sherlock Holmes gave his instructions to the servants. If any visitor were to call asking for Mrs. Hilton Cubitt no information should be given as to her condition, but he was to be shown at once into the drawing-room. He impressed these points upon them with the utmost earnestness. Finally he led the way into the drawing-room with the remark that the business was now out of our hands, and that we must while away the time as best we might until we could see what was in store for us. The doctor had departed to his patients, and only the inspector and myself remained.

"I think that I can help you to pass an hour in an interesting and profitable manner," said Holmes, drawing his chair up to the table and spreading out in front of him the various papers upon which were recorded the antics of the dancing men. "As to you, friend Watson, I owe you every atonement for having allowed your natural curiosity to remain so long unsatisfied. To you, inspector, the whole incident may appeal as a remarkable professional study. I must tell you first of all the interesting circumstances connected with the previous consultations which Mr. Hilton Cubitt has had with me in Baker Street." He then shortly recapitulated the facts which have already been recorded. "I have here in front of me these singular productions, at which one might smile had they not proved themselves to be the fore-runners of so terrible a tragedy. I am fairly familiar with all forms of secret writings, and am myself the author of a trifling monograph upon the subject, in which I analyze one hundred and sixty separate ciphers; but I confess that this is entirely new to me. The object of those who invented the system has apparently been to conceal that these characters convey a message, and to give the idea that they are the mere random sketches of children.

"Having once recognised, however, that the symbols stood for letters, and having applied the rules which guide us in all forms of secret writings, the solution was easy enough. The first message submitted to me was so short that it was impossible for me to do more than to say with some confidence that the symbol XXX stood for E. As you are aware, E is the most common letter in the English alphabet, and it predominates to so marked an extent that even in a short sentence one would expect to find it most often. Out of fifteen symbols in the first message four were the same, so it was reasonable to set this down as E. It is true that in some cases the figure was bearing a flag and in some cases not, but it was probable from the way in which the flags were distributed that they were used to break the sentence up into words. I accepted this as a hypothesis, and noted that E was represented by:

"But now came the real difficulty of the inquiry. The order of the English letters after E is by no means well marked, and any preponderance which may be shown in an average of a printed sheet may be reversed in a single short sentence. Speaking roughly, T, A, O, I, N, S, H, R, D, and L are the numerical order in which letters occur; but T, A, O, and I are very nearly abreast of each other, and it would be an endless task to try each combination until a meaning was arrived at. I, therefore, waited for fresh material. In my second interview with Mr. Hilton Cubitt he was able to give me two other short sentences and one message, which appeared—since there was no flag— to be a single word. Here are the symbols.

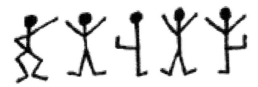

Now, in the single word I have already got the two E's coming second and fourth in a word of five letters. It might be 'sever,' or 'lever,' or 'never.' There can be no question that the latter as a reply to an appeal is far the most probable, and the circumstances pointed to its being a reply written by the lady. Accepting it as correct, we are now able to say that the symbols

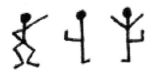

stand respectively for N, V, and R.

"Even now I was in considerable difficulty, but a happy thought put me in possession of several other letters. It occurred to me that if these appeals came, as I expected, from someone who had been intimate with the lady in her early life, a combination which contained two E's with three letters between might very well stand for the name 'ELSIE.' On examination I found that such a combination formed the termination of the message which was three times repeated. It was certainly some appeal to 'Elsie.' In this way I had got my L, S, and I. But what appeal could it be? There were only four letters in the word which preceded 'Elsie,' and it ended in E. Surely the word must be 'COME.' I tried all other four letters ending in E, but could find none to fit the case. So now I was in possession of C, O, and M, and I was in a position to attack the first message once more, dividing it into words and putting dots for each symbol which was still . So treated it worked out in this fashion:—

.M .ERE ..E SL.NE.

"Now the first letter CAN only be A, which is a most useful discovery, since it occurs no fewer than three times in this short sentence, and the H is also apparent in the second word. Now it becomes:—

AM HERE A.E SLANE.

Or, filling in the obvious vacancies in the name:—

AM HERE ABE SLANEY.

I had so many letters now that I could proceed with considerable confidence to the second message, which worked out in this fashion:—

A. ELRI.ES.

Here I could only make sense by putting T and G for the missing letters, and supposing that the name was that of some house or inn at which the writer was staying."

185

Inspector Martin and I had listened with the utmost interest to the full and clear account of how my friend had produced results which had led to so complete a command over our difficulties.

"What did you do then, sir?" asked the inspector.

"I had every reason to suppose that this Abe Slaney was an American, since Abe is an American contraction, and since a letter from America had been the starting-point of all the trouble. I had also every cause to think that there was some criminal secret in the matter. The lady's allusions to her past and her refusal to take her husband into her confidence both pointed in that direction. I therefore cabled to my friend, Wilson Hargreave, of the New York Police Bureau, who has more than once made use of my knowledge of London crime. I asked him whether the name of Abe Slaney was known to him. Here is his reply: 'The most dangerous crook in Chicago.' On the very evening upon which I had his answer Hilton Cubitt sent me the last message from Slaney. Working with known letters it took this form:—

ELSIE .RE.ARE TO MEET THY GO.

The addition of a P and a D completed a message which showed me that the rascal was proceeding from persuasion to threats, and my knowledge of the crooks of Chicago prepared me to find that he might very rapidly put his words into action. I at once came to Norfolk with my friend and colleague, Dr. Watson, but, unhappily, only in time to find that the worst had already occurred."

"It is a privilege to be associated with you in the handling of a case," said the inspector, warmly. "You will excuse me, however, if I speak frankly to you. You are only answerable to yourself, but I have to answer to my superiors. If this Abe Slaney, living at Elrige's, is indeed the murderer, and if he has made his escape while I am seated here, I should certainly get into serious trouble."

"You need not be uneasy. He will not try to escape."

"How do you know?"

"To fly would be a confession of guilt."

"Then let us go to arrest him."

"I expect him here every instant."

"But why should he come?"

"Because I have written and asked him."

"But this is incredible, Mr. Holmes! Why should he come because you have asked him? Would not such a request rather rouse his suspicions and cause him to fly?"

"I think I have known how to frame the letter," said Sherlock Holmes. "In fact, if I am not very much mistaken, here is the gentleman himself coming up the drive."

A man was striding up the path which led to the door. He was a tall, handsome, swarthy fellow, clad in a suit of grey flannel, with a Panama hat, a bristling black beard, and a great, aggressive hooked nose, and flourishing a cane as he walked. He swaggered up the path as if the place belonged to him, and we heard his loud, confident peal at the bell.

"I think, gentlemen," said Holmes, quietly, "that we had best take up our position behind the door. Every precaution is necessary when dealing with such a fellow. You will need your handcuffs, inspector. You can leave the talking to me."

We waited in silence for a minute—one of those minutes which one can never forget. Then the door opened and the man stepped in. In an instant Holmes clapped a pistol to his head and Martin slipped the handcuffs over his wrists. It was all done so swiftly and deftly that the fellow was helpless before he knew that he was attacked. He glared from one to the other of us with a pair of blazing black eyes. Then he burst into a bitter laugh.

"Well, gentlemen, you have the drop on me this time. I seem to have knocked up against something hard. But I came here in answer to a letter from Mrs. Hilton Cubitt. Don't tell me that she is in this? Don't tell me that she helped to set a trap for me?"

"Mrs. Hilton Cubitt was seriously injured and is at death's door."

The man gave a hoarse cry of grief which rang through the house.

"You're crazy!" he cried, fiercely. "It was he that was hurt, not she. Who would have hurt little Elsie? I may have threatened her, God forgive me, but I would not have touched a hair of her pretty head. Take it back—you! Say that she is not hurt!"

"She was found badly wounded by the side of her dead husband."

He sank with a deep groan on to the settee and buried his face in his manacled hands. For five minutes he was silent. Then he raised his face once more, and spoke with the cold composure of despair.

"I have nothing to hide from you, gentlemen," said he. "If I shot the man he had his shot at me, and there's no murder in that. But if you think I could have hurt that woman, then you don't know either me or her. I tell you there was never a man in this world loved a woman more than I loved her. I had a right to her. She was pledged to me years ago. Who was this Englishman that he should come between us? I tell you that I had the first right to her, and that I was only claiming my own."

"She broke away from your influence when she found the man that you are," said Holmes, sternly. "She fled from America to avoid you, and she married an honourable gentleman in England. You dogged her and followed her and made her life a misery to her in order to induce her to abandon the husband whom she loved and respected in order to fly with you, whom she feared and hated. You have ended by bringing about the death of a noble man and driving his wife to suicide. That is your record in this business, Mr. Abe Slaney, and you will answer for it to the law."

"If Elsie dies I care nothing what becomes of me," said the American. He opened one of his hands and looked at a note crumpled up in his palm. "See here, mister, he cried, with a gleam of suspicion in his eyes, "you're not trying to scare me over this, are you? If the lady is hurt as bad as you say, who was it that wrote this note?" He tossed it forwards on to the table.

"I wrote it to bring you here."

"You wrote it? There was no one on earth outside the Joint who knew the secret of the dancing men. How came you to write it?"

"What one man can invent another can discover," said Holmes. There is a cab coming to convey you to Norwich, Mr. Slaney. But, meanwhile, you have time to make some small reparation for the injury you have wrought. Are you aware that Mrs. Hilton Cubitt has herself lain under grave suspicion of the murder of her husband, and that it was only my presence here and the knowledge which I happened to possess which has saved her from the accusation? The least that you owe her is to make it clear to the whole world that she was in no way, directly or indirectly, responsible for his tragic end."

"I ask nothing better," said the American. "I guess the very best case I can make for myself is the absolute naked truth."

"It is my duty to warn you that it will be used against you," cried the inspector, with the magnificent fair-play of the British criminal law.

Slaney shrugged his shoulders.

"I'll chance that," said he. "First of all, I want you gentlemen to understand that I have known this lady since she was a child. There were seven of us in a gang in Chicago, and Elsie's father was the boss of the Joint. He was a clever man, was old Patrick. It was he who invented that writing, which would pass as a child's scrawl unless you just happened to have the key to it. Well, Elsie learned some of our ways; but she couldn't stand the business, and she had a bit of honest money of her own, so she gave us all the slip and got away to London. She had been engaged to me, and she would have married me, I believe, if I had taken over another profession; but she would have nothing to do with anything on the cross. It was only after her marriage to this Englishman that I was able to find out where she was. I wrote to her, but got no answer. After that I came over, and, as letters were no use, I put my messages where she could read them.

"Well, I have been here a month now. I lived in that farm, where I had a room down below, and could get in and out every night, and no one the wiser. I tried all I could to coax Elsie away. I knew that she read the messages, for once she wrote an answer under one of them. Then my temper got the better of me, and I began to threaten her. She sent me a letter then, imploring me to go away and saying that it would break her heart if any scandal should come upon her husband. She said that she would come down when her husband was asleep at three in the morning, and speak with me through the end window, if I would go away afterwards and leave her in peace. She came down and brought money with her, trying to bribe me to go. This made me mad, and I caught her arm and tried to pull her through the window. At that moment in rushed the husband with his revolver in his hand. Elsie had sunk down upon the floor, and we were face to face. I was heeled also, and I held up my gun to scare him off and let me get away. He fired and missed me. I pulled off almost at the same instant, and down he dropped. I made away across the garden, and as I went I heard the window shut behind me. That's God's truth, gentlemen, every word of it, and I heard no more about it until

191

that lad came riding up with a note which made me walk in here, like a jay, and give myself into your hands."

A cab had driven up whilst the American had been talking. Two uniformed policemen sat inside. Inspector Martin rose and touched his prisoner on the shoulder.

"It is time for us to go."

"Can I see her first?"

"No, she is not conscious. Mr. Sherlock Holmes, I only hope that if ever again I have an important case I shall have the good fortune to have you by my side."

We stood at the window and watched the cab drive away. As I turned back my eye caught the pellet of paper which the prisoner had tossed upon the table. It was the note with which Holmes had decoyed him.

"See if you can read it, Watson," said he, with a smile.

It contained no word, but this little line of dancing men:—

"If you use the code which I have explained," said Holmes, "you will find that it simply means 'Come here at once.' I was convinced that it was an invitation which he would not refuse, since he could never imagine that it could come from anyone but the lady. And so, my dear Watson, we have ended by turning the dancing men to good when they have so often been the agents of evil, and I think that I have fulfilled my promise of giving you something unusual for your note-book. Three-forty is our train, and I fancy we should be back in Baker Street for dinner.

Only one word of epilogue. The American, Abe Slaney, was condemned to death at the winter assizes at Norwich; but his penalty was changed to penal servitude in consideration of mitigating circumstances, and the certainty that Hilton Cubitt had fired the first shot. Of Mrs. Hilton Cubitt I only know that I have heard she recovered entirely, and that she still remains a widow, devoting her whole life to the care of the poor and to the administration of her husband's estate.

Made in the USA
Middletown, DE
27 August 2022

72474432R00116